Interview with the Time Traveler:
The 21st Century Marine in 5000 A.D.

Interview with the Time Traveler:
The 21st Century Marine in 5000 A.D.

By Genesis Pilgrim

To the Accessions Commander,

Retrieval achieved near Grid Location 1, Primary Retrograde, Luminary Watchhand. All locations remain under surveillance. Instructions carried out with diligence. Teams secure at this time.

Contents

Introduction by Genesis Pilgrim

I am the first time traveler (to my knowledge) who was imported from the 21st Century to 5000 A.D. As such, I have adequate knowledge of both eras of human history—qualifying me to provide relevant explanations of both time periods to their counterparts. Rather than typing detailed descriptions of the two different societies to one another (which would like escape the comprehension of both), I have elected to do this work through an interview. In the following interview sessions, I dialogue on specific topics.

Mediating information between these two eras in human history will be challenging. The goal is not to withhold information about the "future" from 21st Century humans. Rather, my goal is to explain 5000 A.D. society in a manner that is constructive—perhaps inspiring self-reflection within readers.

This publication exists in different translations for both the 21st Century and 5000 A.D. For each, care has been taken to provide for the common semantics of the respective era. Upon completion of the editing process, I provided my own inputs concerning the structure of the book and the translation of certain terms into forms which can be understood by each intended audience.

To my 21st Century readers,

Some of these interview topics may seem puzzling at first, but give them due consideration. Allow the concepts time to develop within your mind before dismissing them. With reflection, I am confident all can become clearer. In this book, the goal is to examine my own time travel and my perspective on humanity's path forward.

Perhaps the most puzzling aspect of this book may be the identity and description of my interviewer—Kai. Kai's story is something different altogether. To create a temporary bridge adequate for your current understanding, I will offer the following explanation of my interviewer . . .

In 5000 A.D., humans are different in noticeable regard from humans of the 21st Century. Although humans still occupy the base dimensions, being capable and even restricted to 3rd dimension thinking in part—the form of humans has been enhanced to allow for a broader range of abilities. If you were to meet Kai, perhaps you would first notice his differences in physical form . . . but the differences go much, much further.

This is the simplest introductory explanation I can offer to allow a basic conceptualization without overwhelming distraction. In other words, don't get too bogged down by the identity or details concerning my interviewer. (At the end of the book, I provide a complete explanation of the different Kai humans, including: Kai

Moschos-Anthropos, Kai Leon-Anthropos, Kai Aetos-Anthropos and Kai Anthropos-Anthropos.)

My heart is warmed at the thought of you reading this work to consider the topics herein. The main thought: This book is about human redemption. In all its forms, humanity is precious. On every level, we must learn this to move forward—regardless of the time in which we are captured. Allow, rather, this thought to captivate you: There is room for all humans who want to be redeemed from what holds them captive. We need you to step away from the prison which is holding you—to become what you were created to be. Let us help you so you can help us.

My friend, I hope this book is helpful during your journey through time.

I'll see you in the future.

> *Sincerely,*
> *Genesis Pilgrim*

Interview with the Time Traveler

1

The 5000 A.D. Mission of Genesis Pilgrim

"Hello, Genesis Pilgrim."

"Hello."

"It is my pleasure to meet you once again. My name is Kai Aetos-Anthropos. Would you please introduce yourself?"

"My name is Genesis Pilgrim, currently assigned as the Accessions Commander for ancient Israel, circa 2000 B.C. to 300 A.D."

"That is quite a mouthful. Would you explain what you do?"

"Sure. I research historical records to identify past humans with potentially useful skills. You see, throughout human history, humans 'advanced' in some ways, but in other cases we forgot skills once mastered by our ancestors. Our goal is to assess all human history to find humans with pinnacle skills. So, within the Accessions Command, I am one of many Accessions Commanders. Each Accessions Commander surveys a specific block of human history," Genesis pauses, then continues, "At this point in human history, we are rapidly approaching our next Frontiers. During previous Frontiers, we were taken off guard by the challenges presented to us. Rather than being unprepared, it is my desire to scout all human history to import individuals with skills beyond our present capabilities."

Kai chuckles, "It is like the phrase: *It is better to have something and not need it, than to need something and not have it*. Wait, did I say that right?—"

"Yes, you said it right. *It is better to have something and not need it, than to need something and not have it*. That phrase captures the Accessions Command's mission perfectly. As we encounter our next Frontiers, we want to be prepared. By scouting all human history, we will identify individuals with useful skills. Then, once we bring them here, we can appoint them as trainers to instruct our people in their skills. This will ensure we are best prepared for whatever we may face in the next Frontiers."

Kai quipped, "So, in areas where we are blind, we do not want '*The blind leading the blind*?'"

"Geez. Sure," Genesis hesitates, taken aback by Kai's jovial treatment of the subject, "That might be a good way of putting it. This is the way I explain it: As human society 'progressed' we gained certain things, but other things experienced atrophy. This is similar to weight-lifting."

"I don't lift weights," Kai stated dismissively.

As an apt motivator, Genesis addressed the jesting aspect of his interviewer, "Well, you should. Maybe I was imported to motivate you to pump iron. Come down to the jail yard and I'll put you to work lifting brake drums and chains."

As a Marine, Genesis spent his entire youth leading and training men. Whenever they lacked equipment, they would make due with whatever they had. In the case of weight-lifting, Genesis' old team of warriors would use broken parts from trucks for strength training.

Kai laughs. His mind is captivated with the thought of the old pilgrim lifting weights. For a moment, Kai muses to himself then dismisses the thought—being unsure what it means to '*lift chains*.'

As Kai idled, Genesis doubles back to the topic, "When human society progresses, once vital skills become obsolete."

"Example?"

"There are a million. . . . How many people do you know who can forge a sword out of bronze?" Genesis offers shortly.

"I see what you mean. Whereas in ancient societies, the ability to forge bronze swords was a common necessary skill; the later use of other metals rendered bronze obsolete."

"Yes. Forging swords is a relatively lost art," the pilgrim continues, "This is a simple example, but once a person grasps this concept, they are able to see the value in what we do within the Accessions Command."

Kai presses, "So, soon we will see an influx of ancient bronze forgers in our city?"

"Funny," Genesis states reluctantly, then re-captures his thought: "The Accessions process is not about importing people with skills we could learn on our own. For example, in the case of bronze forging, although no one really does it today, we could easily read a book and re-master that skill. So, in 5000 A.D. we do not need an ancient human to teach us how to forge bronze. In fact, many of the ancient skills developed through science are now altogether obsolete—being overtaken by science which is vastly more advanced. Even the most advanced scientific minds from the past would be rendered 'amateur at best' within our society."

"Interesting," Kai reflected, "Then what skills do we need ancient humans for? It seems like we have everything figured out pretty well."

"Not exactly. Those who study history are able to clearly see things when they are brutally honest—completing candid assessments of the strengths and weaknesses of certain societies, groups and individuals. The path to improvement in 5000 A.D. involves us scrounging through every scrap of human history—picking out everything that is helpful. For all we know, the challenges of our next Frontiers may require us to have mastery over a skill held by *one* human who lived isolated on an island 8,000 years ago. We need to look everywhere to make sure we are leaving no human skill un-mastered."

"What is a pinnacle skill?" Kai asked.

Genesis replied, "An example of a pinnacle skill may be the ancient Israelite method of trauma-survival. In my previous book I discuss how the warrior-king, David, developed depersonalization and derealization as internal coping mechanisms—which later transformed Bible faith. This would be an example of a pinnacle human skill—one which we no longer comprehend in its full potential. So, being taught how to survive trauma using the proven method of David would be a thing most useful to our society. This is one example, however throughout human history there are many ancient visionaries who possessed other skills which are likewise useful to us. In some cases, past individuals may have been gifted with a skill they didn't even know they possessed. It is our job to find them."

A moment passes as the two look at one another—both expecting the other to speak. Kai expects Genesis to continue. But Genesis, being a man most comfortable in seclusion, is lost on interview protocol. Nowadays, Genesis only kept company with his constant self-talk—as ubiquitous questions echoed within the corridors of his mind.

Conversation itself was confusing to Genesis. The pilgrim would often muse at the absurdity of conversation in general. Being socially awkward, Genesis grew to envision discussion as a yapping see-saw, or as a senseless cycle of noise making. He would often reflect how conversations would appear to those unfamiliar with human customs—as two creatures face one another, only to take turns making noises at each other.

In the silence of the room, this hilarious thought emerges within the mind of the pilgrim, compelling him to blurt a breath of misplaced laughter. In an ill-fated attempt, Genesis scoffs at himself and shakes his head—supposing his after-expressions will somehow 'explain' his laughter to Kai. They don't.

Moments earlier, Kai was ready to speak, but his thought was dismantled by Genesis' blurt of laughter. Being unsure what to say, and now taken aback at Genesis' awkward laugh, Kai reassembles a professional answer to break the silence, "Genesis, I am always inspired by this view of humanity from visionaries like yourself. My heart is warmed by the thought that everyone throughout history may have a part to play in our future."

Genesis dismisses the personal compliment, "Yes. We need to diligently study human history to pull from it every advantage to prepare for our next Frontiers. It is the only way we can continue to move forward as a society."

Kai's mind is wired to ever interject jokes within conversations. Kai jumps at this opportunity, "I guess you can say: *We can't leave any rock unturned.*"

The pilgrim is accustomed to the leadership style necessary to lead young men with Kai's jovial perspective on life. So, he answers him accordingly . . . lunging at Kai in jest—"I can't deal with this guy right now! I need a break."

The two laugh as the short session comes to an end. Genesis plans to talk to Kai Aetos-Anthropos later. Now is not the right time.

<u>2</u>

The Transport of Genesis Pilgrim

Genesis Pilgrim enters the darkened room. Before him is a misshapen tabletop. Although darkened, it reminds him at first of a sand table terrain model.

Behind the table sits a figure—relaxed, motionless. As Genesis grasps his chair, he disturbs the serene table with a slight movement.

The figure opposite him snorts—as if awakened. Immediately he begins chewing. Genesis supposes the man must have fallen asleep while eating. Awkwardly,

Genesis feels he may be in the wrong room. Genesis squints in a vain attempt to identify the man . . .

"You must be Kai Moschos-Anthropos."

"Yes."

"I am Genesis Pilgrim. I am here for my interview. Will you be performing the session?"

Dismissing the question, Kai interrupts his chewing, "Nice to meet you."

Suddenly lights illuminate the subdued room. Genesis' eyes survey the table—which is spread from edge to edge with various food wrappings in random piles.

"We've met before," Genesis gestures—feeling misplaced, torn between purpose and tact, he speaks further, "Sorry if I interrupted your lunch." . . . A statement rife with professional implication from the Marine leader.

Kai Moschos-Anthropos is unresponsive to Genesis' veiled gesture.

Genesis sits, gently brushing aside food packages before him to allow eye contact with his interviewer. After an ordeal, Genesis is successful in his search— finally seeing Kai clearly between two piles. Thinking of his schedule, Genesis is eager to begin the session. Reluctant to speak further, he surveys the human across from him.

In the now illuminated room, Kai Moschos-Anthropos appears intimidating. Genesis imagines Kai being capable of flipping the entire table, or cleaving it with a single strike.

Kai is powerful in appearance, yet neutral in posture. His shoulders and arms are relaxed. His eyes dart about—alternating from eye contact with Genesis to the various wrappings on the tabletop. It is as if he is searching for something in the midst of the lunchtime rubble, yet refusing to move anything.

Kai snorts loudly—sending an echo throughout the room. As the room falls silent, Genesis' mind breaks it. He assigns purpose to the food wrappers, building a story in his mind—imagining Kai's hunger lurching through the items in a certain order, until finally succumbing to exhaustion from over indulgence. Genesis chuckles at the story in his mind.

"Snort—snort."

Kai snorts again. His snorts work in mismatched concert with his chewing. After a snort, Kai's chewing intensifies, then weakens until the next snort. Genesis reasons Kai may be falling asleep, with the snorts serving to jolt him—similar to how a person with sleep apnea is suddenly awakened.

The silence continues, and the pattern repeats: Snort, darting eyes, incessant chewing trailing off, and eyes slowly closing until the next snort.

Genesis is adept at recognizing patterns, and wary of the things that break them. At first he is intimidated by Kai's reserved strength and size, guarding himself in mental preparation if Kai desired to lunge toward him. Surely, Kai could crush anything in his path.

After observing the pattern for several turns, Genesis drops his guard—content with labelling Kai as a simple guy who is sleepy after lunch.

Genesis reads the room, "If you would like, we can postpone our session."

Silence.

Suddenly, breaking the silence, Kai snorts and gasps, "No, let's do it."

Silence.

Genesis is puzzled, thinking about expectations and roles in the interview. *Is there a piece of paper with questions hidden under piles on the table?* Genesis waits for a moment, then resolves to just start speaking.

He knows the session is being recorded, so he begins to speak on the assigned topic: His import. This is a topic on which Genesis has spent much time reflecting, so he is confident he can talk himself through this topic.

Realization strikes Genesis, compelling his withdrawal from his inner amusement moments earlier— thinking now that Kai Moschos-Anthropos is a person suffering from sleep apnea. Empathy swells within the pilgrim's heart. Genesis does not want to disturb Kai's rest. If Kai is able to fall asleep, Genesis wants to give him respite from his snorting cycle. So, Genesis begins speaking in a quiet rhythm . . .

"In the 21st Century I became adept at recognizing patterns in my surroundings. I found people often dismissed things as coincidences; whereas I was always inclined to view events by assigning purpose. One could say I had a religious confirmation bias, but I tended to accept things from a supernatural perspective—assigning hidden meaning to things I observed."

Following this old pattern, Genesis uses the items of the room to continue his story . . .

"In many cases, one could say the 21st Century was much like this room. Piles and piles of garbage—plastics and whatnot. Chaos spread from one side of the Earth to the other—warfare, suffering. No one could make sense of it. Much like a person drowsy from over indulgence, it seemed all humans were detached—caught in repeated patterns of dozing jolts. Humans in the 21st Century adopted a dopamine-on-demand system by using various screen devices—frying their ability to feel or experience anything real. Everything became garbage, chaos and fake. Even our money was completely fake—not based on anything except the paper it was printed on. Then even the paper was abandoned, and money became only imaginary numbers in imaginary bank accounts. In remarkably insane fashion, people with imaginary numbers were treated differently than those without imaginary numbers. It was truly nuts.

"And in the midst of this 21st Century garbage and chaos I lived. As a young man I was economically compelled to serve in multiple wars—where I came to these realizations: Everything was fake. So instead of becoming fake, I separated myself from it. I began to 'see' things as I desired to see them—looking to the Bible for ancient instruction. After all, at least the Bible is based on real people who suffered through real events. In this way it was vastly superior to anything I found in the 21st Century—where even the money was imaginary."

Genesis stops. Surveying Kai, it appears he has fallen asleep—as evidenced by the lack of the snorting pattern. Genesis smiles—happy Kai is able to rest. Genesis continues.

"At first it was distressing to be so different from other people. I was very isolated. People confused me. I always searched to identify people's motives. It took me many years, but I finally resolved myself to being who I became in war. I spoke to counselors, who encouraged me to simply view life as if I were watching it as an observer. In other words, they encouraged me to embrace the depersonalization aspect of my 'post-traumatic stress disorder,' also known as PTSD in the 21st Century. I let go as many things as I could—embracing the hidden reality behind all the garbage, chaos and fakeness. Once I resolved to do this, things became clearer—ushering me away from these things into a new life. Over the years I forsook more and more of the physical world in preference for the hidden, spiritual reality."

"Snort—snort," Kai suddenly awakens and re-joins the conversation, "So how did you get here, Genesis?"

"Kai, currently I am the only person in our Luminary System who has been capable of time travel.

There may be other humans elsewhere in other Luminary Systems who accomplished similar things, but within our area I am the only one. You may expect me to tell you exactly how I was imported here. In my mind I cannot pinpoint when the transfer took place. After my import, I had many discussions with leaders in an attempt to figure it out. Of course, there are many theories which you could research. But today I can offer you my own thoughts on how it happened . . ." Genesis offers.

Kai nods.

Genesis continues, "When thinking about my 21st Century memories, everything seems like snapshot photographs. I went through the process of recording all my memories and placing them into chronological order as I remember them. Some of my latest memories, I think, involve watching the Sun and Moon above the Earth—paying particular attention to light patterns on the Moon and how they did not correspond to the precise position of the Sun. Many times the shadow on the Moon was straight and stiff, seemingly indicating a level Sun, while the Sun was many hours held beyond the eastern sky. One day I watched the subdued pink Sun in full view—eyes fixed upon it, descending and shrinking away growing smaller for well over an hour. The Sun was completely pale, yet fully visible. At another time I observed the western sky was fully illuminated, while the eastern sky was dark about an hour before sunrise," Genesis pauses, then reflects, "It was indeed a bizarre time. My guess is I was imported around this time in the 21st Century. I think, but am not sure, that I lived my entire life on the 21st Century timeline, then was imported at the end. This explanation makes the most sense because of some of my later memories. After all, this would have provided the least amount of Timeline Interference."

Kai chews, "What's that?"

"Timeline Interference is the unsubstantiated idea that if something is changed in the past it has increasingly consequential effects on all events after it. Many years ago it was referred to as the butterfly effect."

"Got it."

"We do not know for sure though. Concerning my memories, there are gaps between all of them. So, the leaders conclude memory loss or some cognitive impairment may be a symptom of time travel."

"You agree?" Kai snorts.

Genesis shifts in his seat, "I'm not sure. I have an unconventional view of history, so I tend to interpret the memory gaps in that way."

"Huh?"

"It is hard to explain, but I'll try . . . Whenever we think about any memory, what we are really remembering is a collection of our senses in that moment. So, a memory is what you 'smelled + saw + heard + felt + tasted' in a moment. In other words, your brain creates a snapshot of your senses in that moment. This is why certain smells, for example, can remind us of earlier experiences. When we smell something similar, our brain tries to compare it to something we know—so through association we remember. And, when a smell lines up with a memory snapshot in our mind, then we also become mindful of the others senses we experienced in that past moment. So, when we remember something we are really just viewing a mental snapshot."

Kai gasps and exhales loudly, "Interesting."

"Our minds are very interesting. Extending this thought further . . . A memory is not a chronological event. A memory is a snapshot. A memory is just a captured snapshot of our senses at a particular time. Within memories we do not have chronological development. To think of memories as chronological, we need to piece them together separately. This is similar to pasting pictures in a scrapbook. So, memory gaps might just be the result of a 'pasting problem'—not necessarily a cognitive impairment. The more you think about it, the more it makes sense."

Kai demands, "Tell me more."

"In my research on ancient Israel, I developed this concept independently as I reflected on the nature of Bible prophecy. Often when people would read books like Revelation, Daniel and Zechariah, they would be taken aback by the foreign appearance of events. I explain these apocalyptic books by interpreting them as snapshot visions of the Heavenly Universe. In each of these, the prophet describes events as they actually occurred in Heaven. Then, true to form, what happens in Heaven eventually happens on Earth. The heavenly snapshot vision is unfolded and superimposed onto the Earth's chronological timeline. This is why Bible prophecies do not hold to the same chronology as events on Earth—making them seem altogether foreign to humans."

"I see."

"I told you it is complicated," Genesis acknowledges, "But when one extends this snapshot structure to everything, suddenly all things in chronological history make sense. As fallen creatures, humans are forced to think chronologically."

"Why?"

"Any creature that is subject to danger and threats must think chronologically. In other words, to get to the next moment, a creature must survive the previous moment. So, any creature which is subject to potential harm, must constantly think and react within chronological time."

"So time is different?"

"Yes. The perception of time is different. A creature that is perfect in a perfect environment does not think chronologically. They would have no purpose for it. The only reason why creatures think chronologically is for survival purposes. But if a creature is completely safe, and self-assured of safety, it exists outside chronological time."

"*Snort*—Interesting."

"Therefore, we can explain heavenly visions and the pre-fall history of humans. Humans and creatures who are assured of safety in the very presence of God, have no concept of chronological time. Our standard pattern of memory, as snapshots of 'smell + sight + touch + taste + hear' is a remnant of the original, perfected pattern. Once we are safely beyond an event in our chronological past, we are no longer subject to danger within it. Thus, the memory exists only as a snapshot, not as chronological."

Kai is puzzled—his darting eyes focus and his chewing stops.

Genesis presses forward, "In my research I put forward the idea that history itself should be viewed as series of snapshots, rather than chronology. I think this may open our understanding. Rather than interacting with ancient human societies as integrated parts of the whole, we should consider interacting with ancient human societies as isolated snapshot bubbles—with few angelic messenger touch points connecting them to one another. In our path to understanding how the past, present and future connect this may be the best method. Moreover, by doing so, we are simply following the pattern set out for us within our Luminary Systems. All the Luminary Systems appear as independent half-bubbles with few, sometime non-existent, touch points. Discovering previously unknown ancient human societies is similar to the discovery of a new Luminary System. We need precision and bearing to get through the Outer Darkness, and once discovering a new snapshot/bubble we need to understand it for itself. Only then can we map it with the touch points. . . . Actually I need to jot this down. Kai, do you have a pen?"

"Yes."

"Never mind, I found mine in my pocket," Genesis laughs. The pilgrim had a habit of being carried along in the wake of his own thoughts. Often they would transport him to new places. He is truly a traveler in all senses—even within his own mind. Whenever his mind would call his attention to a new thought captured within its corridors, Genesis was eager to capture it on paper. His memory was not the best, so he depended on stacks of notebooks containing his musings—constantly digging back through his anxious scrawling to find messages he wrote to himself.

The room falls silent as Genesis jots down a message to himself on a sheet of paper. Kai chews as Genesis chews further on his thought. The pilgrim's mind would often construct thoughts which he felt did not belong to him. As a part of his pattern, he would constantly seek to incorporate new thoughts within the cohesive worldview stored within his mind. Genesis was always eager to learn new perspectives—even from those with whom he might disagree. Whenever hearing a new perspective, he would research it, writing notes and developing his own theories on the topics.

Throughout his life he ever increased in his prayers for wisdom. At many times his mind would dart and capture thoughts which seemed foreign from within. Nevertheless, as soon as they arrived within, the other thoughts were always hospitable, welcoming the traveler to remain—sharing endless stories and establishing ever-deeper touchpoints.

Genesis sought to understand. Whenever he felt dissuaded from further discovery, the imminent doom ever targeting humanity would beckon him forward. The pilgrim was driven by inner-motivation: If he did not find the answers, no one would. He was convinced humanity was somehow depending upon him. Or, to put it another way: Humans were being drawn to the point where they would depend upon him as at other times they depended upon the wisdom of other leaders.

Genesis digresses and readdresses the interview, "To answer the question for this session, I am not completely sure how I was imported here or why. But I think it has something to do with my decision to set aside the things of the 21st Century—perhaps opening a pathway. Due to the symptoms of my PTSD, from spending years in war, my mind stopped pasting the snapshots of memories. In most cases, my brain stayed in survival mode—being content to simply escape each moment. So, it became natural for me to view all memories as being detached from one another. My brain seldom took time to connect my own memories with my other memories. Because, for me, my own memories held within them a certain danger and my mind actively pursued detachment from them. Therefore, for a man like me, it became quite natural for me to step outside the 3rd dimension cage around me. I learned inner detachment as a survival mechanism, and that dissociation transferred to everything outside of me. This made it possible for me to see all things as fragmented pieces. Although this may be difficult to understand, I think this ability to mentally fragment things, led me to fragment my consciousness from the 3rd dimension onto the 4th dimension. Then, my ability to fragment led me to fragment the 4th dimension one step further into the 5th dimension—pushing me forward chronologically into this Luminary System."

"Interesting—this idea of fragmenting."

"It is, Kai. It has been called other names—such as dissociation, derealization, and depersonalization. To summarize, when a person becomes accustomed to surviving dangerous situations, the task of pasting memory snapshots in a chronology becomes a most unnecessary task. In this type of survival, chronology doesn't matter. All that matters is that you keep putting moments behind you. So, for me, my perception of reality was shattered—leading me to develop the ability to fragment myself and my memories."

"Wow," Kai snorts.

"It is a big realization. It takes a while to understand, but once a person gets it, it makes sense. However, my mind's operation became even more bizarre."

"How?"

"Well, even though my brain developed a deficit for chronological pasting of memories, it somehow transferred that ability to other activities."

"Huh?" Kai coughs.

"Whereas other people usually do well remembering the chronological order of events; my brain does not. But my brain seems adept at tracing out the connections between theories."

"Why?"

"I think my brain has an aversion to things it perceives as dangerous. My memories of each moment appear with the potential of danger, so my brain quickly drops them as fast as I remove myself from each moment. However, when it comes to hearing theories, there is nothing inherently dangerous about them," Genesis moves further to illustrate his point, "It is not like a book can kill me."

Kai and Genesis share a laugh: For Genesis, a smirking quip as he leaned back; for Kai, a chuckle shortly followed by a cough. The behemoth's laughing cough let loose a plume—which appeared to Genesis as a puff of smoke or steam.

As remnants of that moment cleared, Genesis continued, "Within the ability to fragment—or do dissociation, depersonalization or derealization, or whatever you would like to call it—there is danger. It is very difficult to control—as evidenced by my own time travel to this Luminary System. From what I remember, I did not choose to come here, but I was drawn within it. So, although my brain's ability to fragment might have provided the practical means for my time travel, I was not able to control it. Above all, it should be understood that when a person's brain overrides their consciousness it tends to make certain shifts on its own in an attempt to guard the person against perceived danger. I think this is what happened when I was on the Luminary Watchhand in the 4th dimension. My brain must have fragmented me from within, allowing my tilt forward through time."

Kai breathes deeply as he reflects. He feels leveled by the concept of this type of inner transformation. They are such foreign thoughts—considering how a human's brain may develop the ability to separate from itself. Kai resolves to think further on these topics.

Genesis speaks further, "It might be that time travel also requires a willing participant. In other words, the person on the other end whom we intend to import must *desire* to be imported. This may open a touch point to which the time machine can connect. Stealing someone away from their timeline against their will would not be a humane thing. However, if the person is willing during their life, then upon completion of their purpose in their time, it could be that a touch point can be opened— allowing them to step forward. If someone is interested in time travel, this is my best advice: Do your best within the time you have been entrusted. Welcome spiritual transformation and move toward change. Be diligent, realizing human life is not limited by the physical. Be spiritual and avoid the 3rd dimension dead ends of the physical world."

<u>3</u>
Time Travel

"Greetings, Genesis."

"Greetings, Kai Leon-Anthropos."

"I am so thankful I was selected to interview you on this topic."

"What is the topic you would like to discuss today, Kai?"

"Time travel."

" . . . "

Genesis and Kai look at each other. At the mention of this broad topic, Genesis expects Kai to quantify a specific part of the process. Kai, on the other hand, being overwhelmed with the magnitude of the topic and personally unfamiliar, is unsure of the proper order to unpack this assigned topic.

Realizing it is his turn to speak, Genesis tests the waters, "What part of time travel would you like to discuss?"

"As much as possible."

Genesis quips, "Alright, I hope we don't run out of *time* though."

The attempted joke lands awkwardly. Genesis looks at Kai, expecting him to pick up on the irony of mentioning *time* as a limiting factor in an interview discussing *time travel*. At his eagerness, fingering and peering at his notes before him, Kai misses Genesis' flat joke altogether. Genesis waves aside his joke, thinking it was a very 'dad' thing for him to say . . . a lame joke. It is probably best Kai didn't catch it. Genesis was never good at telling jokes anyway.

Kai is eager—wanting to benefit from this conversation with Genesis. So, in excitement, he gives his closing comments at the beginning . . . Kai's finger sticks to a line on the stack of papers before him, "Genesis, I want to be a time traveler. You are the only one I know, so if you could help me, I would like to volunteer for a mission once one is available."

"That is great, Kai Leon-Anthropos. Thank you for volunteering. After this session I will help you to start the process, even though we haven't figured it out and don't have any live missions planned." Genesis' deconstruction of his recommendation—pointing out that no one understands time travel—seemed most ironic: It was funny to consider a recommendation which promises the impossible. Nevertheless, Kai didn't care if it was impossible. He was simply trusting Genesis would somehow figure it out.

"Really!? Thanks, Genesis!"

Waiting for this moment for many years, Kai is filled with excitement. He is unsure of the proper protocol in this situation, inwardly imagining shaking Genesis' hand or giving him a hug in thankfulness. However, Kai resists the temptation—being intimidated by the reputation of the man before him. Kai feels the chair under him. His hands slide above the stack of papers on the smooth table top. Kai becomes anchored again to his purpose in this room . . .

Kai clears his throat and musters his professionalism, having gained his desired recommendation, he focuses on conducting a good, informative interview. After all, he reasons, not everyone has the honor of interviewing Genesis Pilgrim.

Kai moves to the first page of his notes, "Genesis, I would like this interview to provide as much information as possible for our readers. Time travel is an intimidating topic. Can we please start from the beginning?"

"Yes. I realize this is an overwhelming topic. To begin I would like to state I don't have all the answers. Here in 5000 A.D. there is still much we need to discover."

Kai restates Genesis' thought, "You are saying you don't have all the answers."

"Right. But I am happy to explain everything I can from my perspective. Then the reader can investigate further into their areas of interest. I can show you the path, but the person must make the decision to walk it for themselves."

"Okay, that is fair," Kai smiles.

"Yeah, I do not want people quoting me or using me as a grand example. Just listen to my perspective. Think about what I have to say. Then try to see it for yourself. Right now no one is sure what allowed me to move through time. So far I am the only human, or living biological creature for that matter, who has been capable of moving forward or backward in time—to our knowledge."

"I would love to learn how to do this," Kai states enthusiastically.

"Well, although I have been interviewed and examined by nearly every leader in our society, no one has been able to give a definite answer. Many have tried to do time travel, but no one has been successful."

Kai leans forward: "What I find most remarkable is that you were able to time travel without a machine or any other device."

"Yes. For many centuries humans attempted to make every type of machine to do time travel, using just about every imaginable source of power."

The paper slips from Kai's hand, "No matter how advanced we become as a society, it always seems like we are missing something. For me, time travel is a big example of this."

"I think so. As our society prepares for our next Frontiers, my import shows that ancient humans have skills that have been lost throughout the centuries. I think I was moved here as a part of a divine purpose. I am convinced this is much bigger than a single person. God is moving to show people what we are missing. Frankly, ancient people had certain things figured out. Ancient people were much more "advanced" than us in certain ways. As we approach our next Frontiers, we need to find a way to consolidate with the forgotten visionaries and skills of the past. I am convinced time travel is the means through which we will prepare for our upcoming challenges. We need to find more people from the past and bring them here to help us. If we do not, our people will not survive. Or, at least if they survive, they will do so only after some disaster. Our path forward will only be possible through the forgotten skills of the past. I am confident of this."

Kai carefully navigates Genesis' words to make sure nothing is lost, "Please explain your 'confidence.'"

"I think my confidence is based on my movement in time. It is difficult to explain, but when I was moving on the Luminary Watchhand, I 'tilted' forward—allowing me to see further in time. Then I moved into this Luminary System in 5000 A.D. When seeing your 'future' I realized it is contingent on the import of ancient humans with useful skills. This is very difficult to explain because we do not have the words for any of these things."

"I read all your other works where you describe your experiences and perspective. Every time I hear these things it is like I am hearing them for the first time. It is so fascinating."

"Me too," the pilgrim stated emphatically. It was a good joke, yet also hinted at the broken way in which Genesis' mind operated. Genesis and Kai laugh. Their laughter is nervous and giddy as if they are children. Yet they hold within themselves reservation—feeling the heaviness of the topic. They are both filled with reverence, bowing inwardly to the divine mystery of this past occurrence. Genesis is ushered out of his laughter quickly by the realization that unless he figures this out human society will fall. The lives of these humans stand upon his ability to gain mastery over his memories . . .

Genesis continues, "In my life I developed the sentiment that many things are beyond explanation. Many things in life have no answer, and we are left to just find a way to survive and adapt. In this way, I think I became a time traveler. I developed a way to see things as they are and to accept them. I am convinced this is the way I was able to 'tilt' the Luminary Watchhand and move from it into the 'future.' I was not swayed by what I was experiencing—I simply accepted it and adapted within it."

Kai responds, attempting to anchor the conversation with his notes, "Genesis, some of our readers—especially those in the past, will not understand topics like the Luminary Watchhand. Can you please explain this from the beginning, starting with how the world was viewed during your beginning in the 21st Century?"

"Yes. First, I was born in the 20th century A.D.— 1982 to be exact. During my life, extending into the 21st Century A.D., there was no knowledge of the Luminary Watchhand, or any other dimensions beyond the three dimensions: length, width, height."

"What do you mean?"

"Humans then were just physical creatures. They lived based only on what they could see with their eyes or experience physically."

"Wow."

"Yeah. It was very weird. What makes it even weirder is that earlier humans were actually very close to becoming 4th dimension beings."

"How?"

"Earlier humans—which would have been ancient to even the 21st Century humans, were *very* spiritual. They all had deep spiritual beliefs where they constantly thought of unseen things influencing their world."

Kai replied, "Yeah, of course—the spiritual parts of the 4th dimension. Everyone knows that. . . . So, the 21st Century humans stopped believing in the 4th dimension? I don't understand."

"The lack of trauma in their world made them too comfortable. Eventually the comfortable things crowded out their ability to sense the spiritual world around them. Whereas the earlier humans experienced suffering, societies found ways to eliminate suffering. This is a good thing, for sure, but it resulted in people having no need to look to a spiritual world for help. Whereas those ancient societies often felt helpless, and their helplessness guided them to 'see" the 4th dimension; later human societies insulated themselves against all forms of suffering. As a result, many generations were born, lived and died in a world of comforts. Although this was beneficial in a way, it led to widespread human abandonment of the 4th dimension."

Genesis falls silent, stopping in his explanation to make sure Kai is not left behind. Kai jots on a piece of paper and rustles it with his hand. Then he gestures, "Please, tell me more."

"Humans are magnificent creatures. But we have a habit of undoing the progress of the past. This is all connected to the genetic adolescence of humans. When we are approaching adulthood, we all feel compelled by our inner self to strike out on our own, making our own paths away from parents and the preceding generation. This leads humans to find and use new resources, but the negative thing is that humans often forsake the advances made by the previous generations. Then they have to learn for themselves by trial and error. Humans should embrace a model of advancement where they learn from past generations, standing fast on the advancements made—building upon them, rather than forsaking them."

"I see."

"Yes, I know, human psychology is another topic for another day though," Genesis smiles.

"Wh-----"

Genesis snaps his finger to insert an extra point in his assessment, "Sorry to interrupt, but I want to tell you one more thing. In the 21st Century, humans were on the verge of even forsaking the 3rd dimension. So, I refer to the humans of the 21st Century as two-and-a-half dimensional."

"What!?" Kai bites.

Genesis catches the emotion of Kai's response, "Yes, Kai. It was very bizarre. Humans began using screen devices. They used these so much they stopped interacting with each other. So, people in the 21st Century began to lack vertical 'depth,' being concerned with only the length and width of the screen device in their hand. People were zombies. When in a group of people, they would each be staring at screens speaking to other people in other places who were also staring at screens. But when they were physically in a group with those people, they would be staring at screens talking to other people who were also looking at screens," Genesis embellishes the point with repetition as he pretends to look at the table in front of him as if it is drawing him into a trance. Genesis widens his eyes and his mouth gapes—demonstrating to Kai the general demeanor which afflicted the 21st

Century. Genesis concludes, "Overall, the people at this time did everything they could to forsake even the 3rd dimension. They became two-dimension zombies living in an utterly spiritless 3rd dimension reality. Thus, the 21st Century was nearly successful in its obliteration of the 4th dimension. Humans began to think of themselves as mere animals."

Kai grows disinterested in the discussion of 'screens'—being unfamiliar with the term, and the bizarre zombie-like behavior described by Genesis. He kindly attempts to re-direct Genesis' attention away from these weird 21st Century customs. Kai scratches his head, "Genesis that seems like a very confusing time."

Genesis ponders how he may have lost Kai in his last exchange. He considers the future possibility of carefully laying out his thoughts in a coherent way on this topic. The pilgrim senses Kai wants to move forward, so he states, "Well, I think we answered the first question. What's your next one, Kai?"

"Not so fast, Genesis," Kai laughs as he perks up, "We need to discuss how the Luminary Watchhand relates to 21st Century humans."

"Alright. To readers in the 21st Century this will likely make no sense, even though it is common knowledge for us. But for the sake of 21st Century readers, I will explain. If you view the sky as a three-dimension human, you will think you are seeing things that are unimaginably far away.

"You mean the Luminaries and Luminary Systems?"

"Yes, that is what we call them now, Kai. But then they were called stars and 'planets.'"

"Planets?"

"The Luminary Systems used to be called 'planets.' They were thought to be very far away from Earth. The other Luminaries, called 'stars,' were thought to be unimaginably far away on a 3rd dimension model."

"Please explain."

"Kai, I'd rather not. Suffice it to say if one's mind is held captive by mere physical sight, and if they suppose only physical things exist, it is a dead end. Humans become nothing more than animals. The lights in the sky in 3rd dimension thinking are thought to be imaginably out of reach. Then, 3rd dimension thinking pushes God and thoughts of the supernatural even further away. So, mere physical thinking leads only to the imagination of infinite blackness—a hellish void of nothingness where nothing can be reached and no one has any purpose."

"I think I understand," Kai gulped as his eyebrows shifted downward. But Kai didn't understand—not yet anyway.

Genesis reaches up to scratch his forehead. He moves his head so his temple rests momentarily upon his palm. Genesis swallows and breathes in heavily. It seems he is nauseous—struggling to hold something within himself. Being triggered by frustrations in his past life, Genesis now resolves to bypass his previous objection made a moment earlier. He reluctantly decides to speak further on this topic, although his body attempts to restrain him. . . .

"The 21st Century Earth was a 3rd dimension prison. The 21st Century world had a way of drawing away the spirits of people. It was a very dark, void, spiritless time."

Kai slowly nods, not sure what to say.

Genesis continues, "But to address the discovery of the Luminary Watchhand . . . sometime far later in history, humans once again embraced *trauma-based faith*—which led them to reevaluate the teachings of previous generations. In the case of the Luminary Watchhand, spiritual humans once again became capable of perceiving the 4th spiritual dimension. As you know, once this occurred, humans began to perceive items in the 3rd dimension world as being part of a larger item in the 4th dimension world."

Kai adds, "This must be the part which will not be understood by 21st Century humans?"

"Right, Kai. A person with spiritual perception might be able to grasp these words, chew on them mentally and sort through them for themselves. But to the two-and-a-half dimension human, my words will seem mystifying and insane," Genesis continues his thought, "Once someone realizes 3rd dimension items are sometimes, but not always, part of a larger 4th dimension item, one can unlock many things—the Luminary Watchhand being one of them. This is what happened."

"I say go for it, Genesis. I realize you are concerned with explaining things in a way so they can be understood. But I think you should just explain things so people can perhaps benefit from it. You said yourself that there may be readers who receive this book who are able to somehow sort through it and make sense of it. Maybe there is another person like you stuck in the 21st Century who would listen and would like to find their way to us."

"That is a good point, Kai. Well, here goes . . . The Sun and the 'planets' each contain below them their own Luminary System. Viewing them from the 4th dimension, each Luminary System rises and falls on a dark plane—which we refer to as the Outer Darkness plane. The Luminary Watchhand is a 4th dimension link between the various Luminary Systems on the Outer Darkness plane. The Outer Darkness plane moves very high and very low, like a sheet being waved or flapping in the wind. The Luminary Watchhand is referred to by this name because the movement of each Luminary System above its 3rd dimension land is as regimented as a clock, with the motion of the Outer Darkness plane also moving in a predictable fashion. When 'planets' are viewed in retrograde from another Luminary System's land, this means the Luminary Watchhand can be used to travel between those two Luminary Systems. So, from the 4th dimension, the Outer Darkness appears to have many half-bubbles upon it, each consisting of a Luminary giving light to the land below it in a separate 3rd dimension. When viewing the 'planets' without the use of the Luminary Watchhand, they appear as small parts of their 4th dimension whole. Only by transferring to those locations via the Luminary Watchhand can one experience the lands below them in their own 3rd dimension. Each 'planet' is a Luminary which shines light upon the land below it—similar to the Sun's light upon the Earth. The 'planets' and their moons atop their lands behave similar to the Sun and Moon atop their Earth's land. Each moon dances with the primary Luminary above its land, with various other celestial lights existing above each land in each Luminary System."

Kai redirects, "Please explain the Sun's Luminary System to our readers who live within that system."

"To those on Earth, the magnetic center, also known as north, is in the center of the half-bubble when viewed from the 4th dimension. South forms the border, or the outer edge circle around the half-bubble. East and west form concentric bull's eye circles around the North Pole in the center. So from the 4th dimension, you can see the entire Earth in one view—every part of it is visible altogether. Above the Earth, the Sun and Moon move in circle circuits on the east-west lines. Remember, when viewing things from the 4th dimension our vision is not at all hindered like it is in the 3rd dimension."

Kai says, "To us this is basic information, but you don't think 21st Century people understand this?"

"No, they don't, Kai. A 3rd dimension human cannot understand this. Just thinking about it gives me a headache. Spiritual things are just foreign to them. It is very frustrating." Genesis tests Kai, "If I told you more stories about it I might even dissuade you from 21st Century time travel."

"No way, Genesis! I definitely want to be a time traveler once we figure out how to send humans," Kai insists.

Genesis perks up, as if a light bulb illuminated above his head. A realization suddenly arrives within the pilgrim's mind. Genesis quickly shares it with Kai before considering it for himself, "I just thought of how we might succeed at sending someone back in time: Since I was able to move forward in time, you could go to me in the 21st Century to figure out how I did it. Maybe even travel back with me."

"Huh?"

Genesis retreats from his thought—resolving to consider it more fully within his own mind, "We'll figure it out." Genesis smirks, "What else did you want to ask me?"

"A couple more questions . . . How many Luminary Systems are on the Outer Darkness plane?"

"Come on, Kai. No one knows that," Genesis laughs, "On the Luminary Watchhand in the 4th dimension it is difficult to focus on counting. When we are there it seems there is a hidden purpose which hinders some investigation methods. In other words, we are not there to count and write things down." Genesis attempts a different angle to answer the question, "If there is a visible retrograde from a Luminary System then it means further movement is possible. And from each Luminary System's land it appears there are always new retrograde points to explore. Some Luminary Systems do, however, have retrograde Dead Ends—where no additional retrograde is visible. New Luminary Watchhand travelers are warned about this because if they enter a Dead End system, they will remain stuck within that 3rd dimension system until a more advanced 4th dimension traveler can retrieve them. For some points you need to be escorted by a 4th dimension traveler who can move without retrogrades. This is why no one should venture further out than charted areas."

"Genesis, how do you think you were able to time travel from the Luminary Watchhand?"

"The first three dimensions are length, width, height. Although it won't make sense, we can describe the 4th dimension as something like moving 'in' or 'out.' So, I think time travel occurs when a person shifts into the 5th dimension. I like to think of the 5th dimension as a 'tilt' forward or back—but that is just my personal thought. The 5th dimension is completely uncharted."

"So how did you do it?"

"Do what?"

"Time travel from the Luminary Watchhand."

"Something similar to a 'tilt' forward. I remember seeing countless half-bubbles extending without limit on the plane. I went into one of them. I am not sure why this one, or how I moved into it."

"Very cool. How did you see the 'tilt?' I have been on the Luminary Watchhand before and I never saw a tilt."

"In my duties as an Accessions Commander, I note how the PTSD of the ancient Israelite, David, allowed him to 'see' God through the PTSD symptoms derealization and depersonalization. Did you read a copy of that book?"

"I did. I especially enjoyed the part where you discuss how spiritual faith is connected to suffering and trauma. . . . Er . . . *trauma-based faith* as you call it."

"Thank you. Yes, I think I was able to 'tilt' on the Luminary Watchhand by using depersonalization. This is another thing that is difficult to explain, but a person accustomed to trauma is capable of separating themselves from their present circumstances in order to survive. I am convinced I was able to 'tilt' and time travel on the Luminary Watchhand because my mind is capable of separating and seeing beyond my surroundings. So, I simply saw what other people normally don't see and was drawn into it."

"So how are letters and books sent back in time?"

"Although we cannot verify exactly how I time traveled, we were able to use this method to develop a way to send letters and books back in time. Because written material is not living, we do not have to concern ourselves with the pesky detail of making sure it doesn't die on the journey. Thinking of the 5th dimension as a tilt, we were able to stand on the Luminary Watchhand and tilt backwards. Although I am sure we littered a bunch of the Outer Darkness with our misses, some of our letters made it back into history."

"So the Outer Darkness now has a library?" Kai jokes.

Genesis tries to add to the joke, but fails, "Yeah, but nothing is on shelves."

In kindness, Kai pretends he did not witness Genesis' failed joke, "How do you know letters and books made it into the past?"

"We know because Accession Commanders found historical copies while conducting their research on past societies. Eventually we would like to send Task Forces back in time to ensure all our document drops were received at specific times and properly published. But as it is currently, we rely on chance to somehow seed our documents back in chronological history. I go to certain points on the Luminary Watchhand, then cast documents in areas within the 5th dimension 'tilt' where I reason they would have the best chance of being found in the 3rd dimension by ancient humans."

Kai flips to his last page of notes, "It looks like we covered everything I have written in my notes. Thank you for your time, Genesis. I look forward to speaking to you later."

Having received his recommendation from Genesis, Kai Leon-Anthropos is eager to begin studying for his upcoming time travel mission. The information provided by Genesis in this interview has given him much to ponder. Kai stands, moving eagerly toward the door to begin delving further into the topics mentioned by the pilgrim. Genesis notes the growing fire which is stirring within the heart of Kai Leon-Anthropos.

"Thank you, Kai. Until next time, friend."

4

Introduction to the 3ʳᵈ & 4ᵗʰ Dimensions

"Hello, Genesis."

"Hello, Kai Leon-Anthropos, it is good to meet with you again. I hope things are going well with your research."

"My research is going well. Thank you for your recommendation, Genesis. I am looking forward to going . . . once we get it figured out, that is," Kai says as he deconstructs his thought.

Genesis smiles and nods—not sure of the appropriate thing to say. Time travel is still a grand mystery, and Genesis holds this concept with reverence within his mind. Through his nod, Genesis sees a brief mental image of Kai's journey. He has a habit of suspecting the worst as a part of his PTSD, so he cannot help thinking of the possibility that Kai may not survive his upcoming trip. Genesis buries the thought quickly as Kai breaks the silence . . .

"Genesis, last interview I know we covered all of my notes. However after reviewing the session I came across a topic I think could use more explanation."

Genesis quips, "So you mean I wasn't able to explain everything about the 4th dimension and time travel in one sitting?" The joke lands well, with Genesis finally evoking a response from Kai.

Kai feels compelled to release a sigh hinting at laughter. His mind has grown much more serious since their last meeting. In this room, Kai is determined to move forward on his journey of discovery—setting aside all things which could hinder him.

"Yes, Genesis, I need you to explain more about the 3rd and 4th dimensions—specifically how they integrate with one another." Kai has a personal interest in this topic, so he musters all his professionalism. He realizes he has this session as a fleeting opportunity to glean wisdom from the only time traveler he knows—or anyone knows for that matter. In anticipation, Kai moves his pen to the paper, preparing to capture his reflections on Genesis' words.

Genesis senses Kai's serious demeanor. He realizes Kai has arrived today as a student, being prepared to learn from a teacher. Genesis, having a knack for seeing pictures in his mind cannot help to think of Kai as a young grasshopper martial artist who seeks to quickly grasp the pebble out of the master's hand. Genesis thinks of the black belt he still wears around his waist—a lone remnant of his martial past as a U.S. Marine many, many centuries earlier. In the past he bore different burdens for the sake of others. Now he bears the martial responsibility of building the minds and spirits of those who look to him as their instructor. His tools and weapons are no longer confined to the 3rd dimension. His mind is free, and he speaks as a lone pilgrim who broke free from the past.

He realizes this session will compel him to once again declare the 'unseen'—realizing some readers might not respond favorably. In his past life, Genesis grew weary of speaking to those whose minds were held captive. He moves to his mental anchor point: Out of habit, Genesis' right hand grasps for his wedding band— spinning it around his finger, remembering his wife and his family. Genesis shakes free within his mind as his body falls motionless. The only sign of the inner struggle is revealed in the welling of tears in his eyes, however subdued from departure.

Genesis feels like a man long lost and forgotten. He senses that he was pushed away from the 21st Century, rather than choosing to move from it. He still bears deeply within himself that sense of rejection he carried for so many years. Even though he was a new man, in a new time, he still carried scars which were very deep indeed . . . thousands of years deep, and most grievous. In his reading he often related to Joshua in the book of Zechariah. He felt as if he were often accused by the ghosts of those standing near him in the 21st Century. And emerging from those many years of rejection, Genesis indeed felt like a burning stick snatched from the fire.

He felt as if he barely escaped—somehow . . . being rejected to the uttermost by his first generation, only to be found as an incomparable blessing to his second generation of people. Whereas the 21st Century people closed their ears, refusing to hear anything; the 5000 A.D. people intently listened to everything. So, within himself, the pilgrim bore this duality of tragedy and exultation: a grievous failure amidst great hope. There was such great loss in the first; yet there is now such great hope present in the second. It seemed as if the memory of tragedy and loss remained only to spur him forward in this time. Every time he felt inclined to cease pursuit, the threat of past tragedy repeating itself called him to press further. As he wondered, Genesis considered it may be the pain of the past within his mind which serves to prevent tragedy in the future.

As his hand grasps his ring, Genesis' consciousness reemerges, finding his eyes locked in gaze with the eager Kai before him. Genesis surveys Kai— holding his pen in ready position above his paper, intent on capturing the next word as it is formed in Genesis' mouth. The pilgrim realizes he now sits before one who wants to learn—who wants to listen.

His mind awkwardly associates the wedding band with Kai—realizing he is now in the presence of a person who also loves him and wants to listen to him. The connection is there and makes sense, and Genesis shrugs to himself—conceding he is in a place of acceptance where he can speak freely, regardless of how his words may be perceived by the 3rd party of 3rd dimension people three-thousand years earlier.

Kai sees the shrug of Genesis. In his past meetings with the pilgrim, Kai and others often noted Genesis' odd social habits. From time to time, Genesis would burst out laughing, then say aloud he was laughing at himself. In this setting, Genesis appears agitated, moving his wedding band, shrugging and remaining silent—even though he has been welcomed to speak.

Kai and others noted at times Genesis needs several prompts to pull him out of the deep expanses of his mind—where he retreats often. He appears always in pursuit of something buried within his mind, only coming up for air at times, similar to the emergence of an ancient whale from the depths of the ocean. Doubtlessly, these inner retreats of the pilgrim are the source of his great power—a power which still baffles the most intelligent. Whenever he retreats or falls silent, Kai and the others became more reluctant to interrupt his inner process— afraid they may disturb a vital discovery, thereby dooming all those who now depend on Genesis. So, the common habit they developed was to 'wait and continue waiting' if ever the pilgrim retreats. When his mind surfaces to the conscious world, his words are as grand as the emergence of a giant whale, bellowing up to the surface. The people of 5000 A.D. listen intently and read his words voraciously. Although his thoughts are fragmented, they are viewed like pieces to a puzzle. The people of 5000 A.D. are thankful for any information they can receive—even if it seems at first unnecessary or disjointed.

Genesis speaks, "Well I could begin by discussing the 3rd dimension. I will try not to repeat things we discussed in our last session."

"That sounds great, Genesis! Any information you can give us will be helpful."

"Okay, as we all know today, the three dimensions are length, width, height. Different people say them in different ways and different orders. But that is what they are: the three measurements of physical things. Although it doesn't make sense to those unfamiliar with it, the 4th dimension could be described as 'in' or 'out.' The 4th dimension is similar to an ability to focus. So, a person with 4th dimension ability can sort of zoom in and out on 3rd dimension things—getting a full picture of things as they 'truly' exist. This means 3rd dimension things, or things we can see with our physical eyes, may in fact be part of a much larger 4th dimension thing. This is not always the case, but it can be."

"Like the Luminaries, er . . . uh, 'planets' as you called them."

"Yes. What we used to call 'planets' in the 21st Century are now called Luminary Systems. And when viewing them from the 4th dimension we see they are actually part of a much larger structure."

"Like the Sun and Moon, right?"

"Yes, just like the Sun and Moon and the Earth below them. From a distance the Sun and Moon are the greater and lesser lights of their own Luminary System. The Earth appears as a great expanse of land at the bottom of the half-bubble—as viewed from the 4th dimension."

Kai adds, "The other day, after our conversation, I was able to go out on the Luminary Watchhand. I viewed the Sun's Luminary System from a distance."

"Grand, isn't it?"

"Absolutely magnificent. It looks completely different in the 4th dimension than it does in the 3rd dimension. Since I knew I would have the privilege of speaking with you again further, I wanted to see again for myself the Luminary System where you lived, Genesis." Kai realizes how difficult social situations can be for Genesis, so he offers his comment as a kind social gesture, venturing to beckon Genesis to speak more deeply on these topics—even if his past is still raw in his mind.

"You are kind, Kai."

Kai smiles and returns to his frantic writing— perhaps seeking to capture his reflections before they escape his mind. As an Accessions Commander, Genesis was well known by his many subordinate leaders for requiring them to always be prepared to take notes on his words. He did not like to repeat himself. By writing, Kai was confident he could gain the favor of Genesis.

He was right. Genesis always preferred to speak to people who were writing, rather than having to maintain eye contact with groups of people.

Realizing his words are valued by Kai, Genesis continues, speaking slowly to give Kai opportunity to write. . . .

"In the distant past, people were on the verge of becoming 4th dimensional through their spirituality. In other words, people began to 'walk by faith, not by sight.' But, as I said earlier, they stopped. Humans became restricted to 3rd dimension thinking. As a result, the Sun's Luminary System became their invisible prison—a place they could not leave without understanding why. This is the tragedy of 3rd dimension thinking: It abandons people within merely physical experience. To us today, this is most bizarre, after we have recaptured some of the 4th dimension thinking used by very ancient, spiritual humans."

"So what did the Sun's Luminary System look like to the 3rd dimension humans living in it?"

"You mean in the 21st Century—where I lived?"

"Yes."

"Very different than how we see it through the 4th dimension."

"How so?"

"Well, the people in the Sun's Luminary System thought they were living on a 'planet.'"

"What!? You mean they thought they were living *on* a greater Luminary?"

Genesis receded, doubting his ability to articulate these concepts to Kai, "No. . . . Now I am beginning to regret this."

"Please explain. I want to understand."

"Okay. . . . The people in the 21st Century believed themselves to be on a three-dimensional ball of dirt and water."

Kai sets down his pen. He moves his hand to his chin, "On a ball? Not a half-bubble on the Outer Darkness?"

Genesis retreats, regroups and attempts his explanation again. . . .

"Okay let me start from the beginning. You know how we see the 4th dimension Outer Darkness as a rising and falling plane?"

"Yes."

". . . And how we think it to be endless—or at least further than we can ever see from the Luminary Watchhand?"

"Of course."

"Well, in the 21st Century, 3rd dimension humans thought of all things existing in something similar. But instead of the Outer Darkness plane we see in the 4th dimension, they believed in a three dimensional 'outer space' stretching endlessly in all directions. What we call the Outer Darkness plane, they called 'outer space.'"

"How did they see 'outer space'? Where is it now?"

"The way it was imagined in the 21st Century—it never existed." Genesis adds, "Outer space was portrayed as an endless vacuum where giant balls, the size of Luminary Systems drifted endlessly. Sometimes they would crash into things, but mostly they just circled around each other. In 21st Century thinking, all the Luminaries were also thought to be giant balls of gas— also drifting in circles around one another."

Kai leans back in his chair, seemingly abandoning his notetaking, concentrating—trying to wrap his brain around the topic. Seeking to relate the foreign concept of 'outer space' to what he knows, Kai asks, "Is 'outer space' like a bowl of water, and the Luminaries like bubbles in it?"

Genesis chuckles to himself, intent on lightening the intensity of the conversation . . . "No, Kai, 'outer space was thought to be nothing. No gas, no water— nothing."

"So how did the Luminaries float and drift if they were not held up by something?" Kai extends his thought, "How can 'nothing' hold up balls of dirt as big as Earth?"

"It didn't, Kai. That is the thing which was so frustrating: People thought it did, and they were never able to see for themselves, so they just kept thinking it did. It was a very frustrating time to live."

Genesis paused, then continued, seeking further to lighten the conversation through a personal appeal, "Soon, once you get your wish, Kai. I am sure you will find out for yourself how frustrating it is."

Genesis laughed at his jovial poke toward Kai's goal of time travel.

Kai looked appreciative of the gesture. Before the poke, he was lost in contemplation. The well-placed joke from Genesis landed well, gently guiding Kai to ponder this information, yet not to get too bogged down on irrelevant details concerning ancient cultures.

Genesis waited for a moment. Realizing Kai had nothing to say, he continued, "For the 3rd dimension humans of the 21st Century, the Sun's Luminary System was indeed a prison. No human could escape from it. Just as we know now, the only way of escape from a Luminary System is through the Luminary Watchhand. To use the Luminary Watchhand, one must have both 4th dimension ability and also have knowledge of how to use retrogrades for travel."

Kai emerges, "Genesis, please explain how people in the Sun's Luminary System, er . . . on Earth, viewed the Earth."

"The people thought of the Earth as a giant ball of dirt, moving in a huge circle around the Sun. The Sun was also thought to be a ball—but more accurately as an immense ball of gas. Then, what we now refer to as the Luminary Systems, were called 'planets.' The 'planets' were thought to be balls of dirt like the Earth. And those were also thought to be moving in circles around the Sun." Genesis checks to make sure Kai is keeping up, "Did I lose you yet?"

"No, I'm good, boss. Please continue," Kai stated with reluctance as he scribbled in haste. From Genesis' vantage point across the table it appeared Kai was drawing circles all over on his sheet of paper. The pilgrim waited for Kai's circle-making to slow, then stop before he continued. Kai looked up, realizing Genesis was waiting for him to stop. At this thought, Kai gulped lightly and smiled nervously—signaling the pilgrim once again held his attention.

"Writing in Singhalese?" Genesis jested. He couldn't resist the temptation and the germane reference to his 21st Century experiences—even though it was unlikely Kai would know what he was talking about.

"Huh?"

"Never mind," Genesis laughed. The diversion of circle-writing was a welcome one. It served well in lightening the conversation. As Genesis leveled out from his laughter, he peered across at an even more confused Kai. It appeared as if Kai were close to bursting—having no idea about any of these things, being reduced to child-like circle drawing on a sheet of paper. Genesis considered asking Kai if he would like some 'crayons.' But being convinced it would likely push Kai beyond his mental breaking point, he digressed.

"The 3rd dimension people on Earth could never leave Earth. We know this is impossible. The half-bubbles of each Luminary System do not allow it. Anything that goes up . . . even the most powerful rockets . . . would arc back down." Although he was successful at continuing the conversation, Genesis could not remove from his mind the hilarious vision of the physically impressive, futuristic Kai coloring circles with crayons. And he thought, if he gave Kai crayons, he would also have to give him a juice box and Goldfish crackers.

Kai interrupted Genesis' spiraling self-talk, "What about moving straight out of a Luminary System, to the border of the half-bubble then out? . . . Come to think of it, has anyone ever done that? I never thought about that before."

"Kai, the half-bubbles of the Luminary Systems all meet the Outer Darkness plane. The entire edge of each Luminary System is circled by Outer Darkness. I know for certain there has never been a human capable of a journey straight out of a Luminary System. It is not possible—at least at this time. If it were to be attempted, a human would need to head away from the magnetic center of their Luminary System, continuing to travel south, then proceed further south from there. I am not sure a 3rd dimension human could even perceive further south beyond the southern-most points of a Luminary System. I'll have to look into this further," Genesis ponders, "But even if they could, a human would not be able to traverse the Outer Darkness to make it to another Luminary System. As we know, the Outer Darkness plane rises and falls to incredible levels. A person on foot, or in a ground vehicle, would not be capable of moving at any predictable speed because of the fluctuations. As they moved forward on the Outer Darkness plane, the incredible rising and falling would likely take them off course. Plus, there are many more problems: We do not know what the environment of the Outer Darkness is like, what creatures are present, or even the nature of the terrain. We suspect the Outer Darkness provides a source for subterranean water and lava from underneath the surface of the lands in each Luminary System—but I digress. All these unknown factors would make the traversing of the Outer Darkness plane altogether impossible, even for a 4th dimension human who could see it."

"Good point, Genesis. Since the only people who can see the Outer Darkness are 4th dimension humans and those with them, and since the 4th dimension humans have access to the Luminary Watchhand, why would a 4th dimension human ever attempt to cross the Outer Darkness?"

"Lewis and Clarke might."

"Who are Lewis and Clarke?"

"Never mind . . . I was a couple thousand years late on that one."

"Gotcha. Were they ancient discoverers?"

"Explorers to be exact. But now that I mention it, it might not be a bad idea if I try to scout some expert explorers from the past who might be bold enough to chart the Outer Darkness . . ."

"You are always thinking ahead, eh Genesis?"

"Yes," Genesis laughs, then shifts in his mannerisms—indicating he is about to pose a personal question: The pilgrim snaps his finger, then waves it in Kai's direction—as if funneling the full weight of this responsibility in a grand heap upon the young man seated across from him . . .

"Kai, by any chance would you be interested in leading an exped---"

"Don't even think about it, Genesis! I'm not travelling into the Outer Darkness for anyone!"

"Ah, it won't be that bad. I'll give you a flashlight and extra batteries."

"I'm going to be quiet now, sir, before I get myself signed up for something I'll regret."

Genesis and Kai share a laugh, and each take a drink from the cups in front of them. First Genesis, then Kai follows his cue.

"Alright," Genesis states within an anticlimactic sigh—signaling he is ready for Kai's next question.

Kai flips a sheet of paper, "I would like you to discuss more about the 'planets.' Our 5000 A.D. readers will be particularly interested in this topic."

"Sure, as I said, in the 21st Century, the planets were thought to be balls of dirt suspended in nothing, moving in circles around the Sun—which was thought to be a huge ball of gas. For a long time, quite sadly, the 3rd dimension humans were held captive by their lack of spirituality. It was the lack of spirituality which hindered these ancient humans. At the time I lived, the 'planets' were thought places where rockets could travel, taking many, many years to get there. And the 3rd dimension humans, having no personal means of evaluation, were mentally imprisoned—being totally dependent on photographs shown them from their governments," Genesis reflects further, "It was not like today, where I can grab someone's hand to bring them with me to the Luminary Watchhand where they can see it all for themselves. Rather in the 21st Century, 3rd dimension humans depended on their government to show them pictures. And being good citizens they would believe in what was shown them in the photographs. It is another topic for another day, but it is quite easy to maintain people in deception once you get them there. In fact, those who are adequately deceived will actually promote and defend the deception unwittingly—not realizing they are actually deceived. Humans are very easy to psychologically manipulate. However, we cannot be deceived in this regard anymore due to the use of the Luminary Watchhand. The 4th dimension lets us all see for ourselves."

"Talk to me about the photographs."

"Kai, this will sadden you greatly. Today, although I am far removed from that time in history, the events are still raw for me. Like I said, before the development of the 'outer space' concept, there were many groups of ancient humans who were on the verge of becoming 4th dimensional through their spirituality. In this way, religion was remarkable in propelling humans into the understanding that there is a world beyond their world. What was once thought of as the realm of angels, we now recognize as the 4th dimension. Of course, we acknowledge still a higher dimension—the 5th dimension, through which I think time travel is achieved, and was achieved by me unwittingly," Genesis pauses, then reflects further, "Who knows how many dimensions there are? I reckon there may be a countless amount leading up to the footstool of God the Father."

Kai adds, "However many there are, I desire to help us find them."

Genesis smiles, "Me too, Kai. Not for the sake of pride, but for human growth. Just as the 4th dimension helped us to dispel falsehood and gain wisdom, I am looking forward to the discovery of more truth."

Genesis' pace in delivery quickens, his words now seeming to be delivered to the beat of a battlefield drum from a now ancient land. He speaks with conviction and power—an unseen, ethereal power which mysteriously beckons the spirits of people who hear. His words charm and empower, as if he uses a supernatural instrument heard by others through a long-lost sense . . .

"Kai, I want us to leave behind the bad things of humanity, bring together the good things, and move forward as a community. That is the mission assigned to Accessions Commanders. We need to get those humans from the past who can help us in our quest to discovery. Like a great puzzle, I am convinced all ancient societies held a piece of the big picture. We need to find all the puzzle pieces. Once I figure out who they are and where to find them, I will need brave team leaders like you to go back in history to bring them to us," Genesis smiles again at the young man across from him. Kai is strong and eager—with the vigor of a man barely into his years of adulthood. As it often does to those near him, the words of the pilgrim now catch within the spirit of Kai—an ancient electric power surge of inspiration fills him.

Kai feels a fire in his heart, sending a wave of power into his arms, neck and mind. His vision tightens as he senses the focus which will be needed to accomplish his future missions—whatever and wherever they may be. In response to Genesis and the inward surging of his heart, Kai answers with, "*Oorah!*" Kai has heard much of the U.S. Marines whom Genesis Pilgrim led in his former life. He always wanted to say this word of motivation, and felt inspired to do so before the time traveler before him. He desired to fill his shoes—to be a chosen, elite warrior from among his people.

Genesis feels a kinship with Kai in his response, and compelled by many years of tradition and the fire now surging in all corners of the room, echoed Kai's word, "*Oorah!*"

Genesis continues without missing a beat—just as for many years he would continue to shout over the boom of gunfire. The supernatural fire of Kai's heart passing through the room inspires Genesis, yet does not at all distract him from his discussion, "Back to the photographs of the 'planets.' In the 21st Century, governments had organizations in charge of 'outer space,' similar to how Accessions Commanders are in charge of accessions planning. The government organizations would tell the 3rd dimension people they had sent rockets which landed on 'planets.'"

Kai settles, "For what?"

"They told the humans they were gathering samples of rocks, finding water and so on."

Kai is taken aback, "Picked up rocks *from* the Luminaries?"

"Yes."

Kai clarifies further, still unsure whether he is misunderstanding or if Genesis is telling a joke . . . "You mean they would say that rocks were *on* the Luminaries and they *picked them up*?" In his delivery, Kai removes pen from page, pointing it toward Genesis—as if to ransom him to tell the truth.

Frankly Kai had never heard such things—that Luminaries could have physical items, like rocks and water, resting upon them somehow. For Kai, this was a most bizarre thought. He felt childish in this room—being so uncertain of past generations of humanity that he was basing his opinion solely upon what he was being told by Genesis.

Genesis answered, "I told you this would not be easy to understand, Kai. Yes, that is what they told them. It turns out the photographs were just pictures of Earth in deserts and whatnot. Then they would put different light filters on their cameras, and change the backgrounds. The 3rd dimension humans believed everything, and nothing you could say would convince them otherwise. From time to time, a photograph would accidently have a mushroom or something like that in it. Of course, the government 'outer space' organizations would find ways to explain away why pictures of 'planets' thought uninhabitable and incredibly faraway would have identical mushrooms to Earth. But all of this is quite easy to understand. When one is psychologically held captive and cannot see things for themselves, it is very easy to keep them that way. Once you convince the first generation of humans, the following generations will be easy to maintain. It is very sad what humans have done to each other."

Kai nods for Genesis to continue. Kai is mystified by these thoughts. Within this young man a desire for truth grows as he resolves to research these things for himself.

Seemingly unaware of the process stirring within Kai, Genesis continues: "Some of the rockets sent into 'outer space' were said to have great cameras—which they used to take pictures of stars, which were said to be incredibly faraway."

"Stars?"

"Stars are the patterns of light viewed from the ground under Luminary Systems—no different than our understanding of stars today."

"Gotcha, so it is not like the 'planet' fiasco."

"Nope. The stars of the 21st Century are just called 'stars.' The major difference though is that the star markings inside each Luminary System differ from the star markings inside other Luminary Systems."

"Obviously, or else they wouldn't be a Luminary System."

"Yeah—hence the name. . ." Genesis chuckles—thinking the absurdity of him having to use the 5th dimension just to find another person who can understand what he is saying. Of course there were others who understood, but Genesis often enjoyed his hyperbolic self-talk—where he imagined the most extreme scenarios. For him, in this moment, he was drawn to Kai, imagining only he and Kai had the answers, and everyone outside this room is nuts. He backtracked in his mind as he blurted another laugh. Now, however, the second laugh was displaced by an awkward silence.

Kai waits patiently as Genesis finally realizes he should still be speaking.

Genesis continues, "The photograph rockets would take pictures of faraway star clusters—which of course no one could see for themselves from their 3rd dimension prison. The photographs showed all these ridiculous colors. At one point they even had a photograph they claimed depicted the far off throne of God."

"You mean God Himself? . . . *The* God?"

"Yeah, it just keeps getting crazier though. In the 21st Century, there was a company that made cartoons—

67

little drawings for children for entertainment . . . mostly cute animals doing funny things."

Kai jests, "I hope it wasn't a government company."

"Haha," Genesis says sportingly, "No, not officially. But, wait for this, there was a 'planet' that had the same name as one of their cartoon characters—Pluto to be exact. Kai, do you want to guess what they did, or do you want me to tell you?"

"Oh no . . . please tell me they didn't."

"They did, Kai. They put him right on the 'planet' itself—a shadow spanning nearly the entire thing. In later photographs they scrubbed it, but yes, they sure did. In the 21st Century, deception was rampant and those holding the power absolutely reveled in it. Those captured within the half-bubble were trapped by 3rd dimension thinking. They remained so though public indoctrination which taught them to forsake spirituality and think of only physical things. This was effective in making sure no one could see anything for themselves. The Luminary Watchhand was out of reach, with only whispers of the 4th dimension. Yet no one payed attention. All the voices of reason were over-crowded by constant nonsense. The death stroke to 3rd dimension humans was when they forsook spirituality and regressed back into the 2nd dimension. People became consumed by two-dimensional screens. Humans became inseparable from the screens of devices which became inseparable parts of themselves. Each human became subject to unceasing programming—

designed to keep them spiritually sedated and asleep. As this shift occurred in the 21st Century it ensured these two-and-a-half dimensional humans would never discover the 4th dimension. The 21st Century was a check-mate: Humans became technological animals, rather than spiritual beings."

"I can see this is tough for you, Genesis," Kai was so confused by the discussion of this ancient society. As he saw tears welling in the eyes of the pilgrim, Kai was distressed. When thinking about the incredible perception of Genesis, he thought it must have been torturous for him to witness firsthand the spiritual deprivation of humanity—being helpless to stop its descent. Suddenly, Kai thought of Genesis as a powerful man attempting to grasp and hold a megalith sliding ever faster toward a cliff. In his first generation, it simply was impossible for Genesis or any other visionary to halt the descent of humanity.

The pilgrim continued, "Yes, it was terrible watching everything crumble in front of me. Being one of the very few voices of reason in the midst of an epic disaster was devastating for me. I am still not sure when I left, or exactly how I left, but I am convinced I was perhaps taken at just the right time. I was permitted to stay long enough to feel the sting so I can be of use to the people here. I know what it is to see humanity forsake itself. Now, I will do everything I can to prevent our humans here from suffering a similar fate. We are going to fix it with the help of God. I know God has provided us all we need. We just need to have faith, think and carefully assemble the pieces."

"Genesis, you mentioned it is easy to deceive 3rd dimension humans. In our society, many of us are still not capable of seeing the 4th dimension without assistance. Can you please explain how the 3rd dimension people of your time were deceived?"

"Yes. It is important to reflect on how psychological deception can occur. Perhaps I will write more on this topic in detail. Speaking specifically about 'outer space' in the 20th and 21st Centuries, I can give you some details on how this happened—right off the top of my head. . . . There were two large wars between many human governments in the 20th Century. After the wars, the governments made promises to one another to avoid future war. However, in the aftermath, two of the biggest governments were in competition with one another. Although they had a truce and did not fight against one another, they continued to compete in ideas and other ways. At this time, the concept of 'outer space' gained in popularity. The two biggest governments used 'outer space' as an area of competition. Knowing what we do now . . ."

". . . That 'outer space' never existed . . ." Kai finishes Genesis' sentence.

"Yes," Genesis agrees, "after a series of escalating photographs and videos, each depicting that the governments were getting further than their competitor, the one government went for what they supposed would be their coup de grace. The government produced a video—actually several videos over several years, promoting the idea that humans travelled to the Moon in a rocket, landed, walked around on the Moon, then travelled back to the Earth."

"I think I heard about this before. Similar to the other things you were saying about the other 'planets'?"

"Very similar."

"Also ridiculous—especially when seeing the Moon from the Luminary Watchhand."

"No kidding. Yet, remembering that the people in the 20th Century were all 3rd dimensional, they had no choice but to accept what was shown them on television screens."

"So, the 3rd dimension people believed in the two-dimensional screen?" Kai scoffs. He cannot contain himself at the irony contained within Genesis' retelling.

Genesis sighs, "The 3rd dimension humans who centuries earlier were on the verge of becoming 4th dimensional through their spirituality, were duped by a two-dimensional device. In this case, human history became an absolute tragedy. And more tragic—once humans entered this belief by allowing it to remain unchallenged for a generation, it became an inseparable part of our societal fabric. People, being removed from the event itself, unquestionably held to it as a point of national pride. Of course, some denied the Moon landings, but they were not successful in swaying the deeply seated psychological bait-and-switch. Humans gave up the wisdom of the 4th dimension in preference for the 3rd dimension. They slowly receded further into the prison of two-dimensional devices. Remarkably, during my time people would even declare screen technologies as our future. So, these false prophets of the time would preach for the 2nd dimension, while visionaries like me yearned for the 4th." Genesis reflects further, "People just did not, and could not, understand. Spirituality became lost. Even those who spoke out for spirituality were often veiled peddlers of 3rd dimension thinking—they became modern revivalists of snake oil doctors. The loudest voices were amplified to drown out the still, small voices of reason. The pathway to the 4th dimension was lost among our societies, and those in positions of spiritual power offered only gas-lighting and smoke and mirrors."

"You lost me, Genesis."

"Sorry for the tangent. Maybe sometime we can go back and discuss some of the last things I said. Suffice it to say, the 21st Century experienced a psychological and spiritual collapse. At the center of it all was the promotion of a now recognized false concept—'outer space.'"

"You know what I was thinking? Maybe next time, we could discuss the different Luminary Systems. It might be very helpful to 21st Century readers."

"Maybe, Kai."

"Genesis, what happened to fix things from the 21st Century? Since the people abandoned discovery of the 4th dimension, how did they climb back out of the two-dimensional hole they dug?"

"I might not be the best person to answer that question. . . . Come to think of it, I might not be the best person to answer any of these questions," Genesis sneers at his cleaver joke. He was fishing . . . fishing for a compliment.

Zing! . . . Kai was hooked, "No, Genesis, you are a good person to answer these questions. You did a good job."

Genesis still did not put himself above the need for occasional praise. It felt good to get a compliment from Kai.

Genesis continues, "Concerning the emergence of 4th dimension thinking from the remnants of the 21st Century and beyond, I believe the other Accessions Commanders may be better to interview on those topics. My area of assignment includes ancient Israel. I have requested to take control of the 21st Century as well, considering my time travel puts me in the best position to address that era of human history from personal experience. But, if you are interested in learning more about 2100 A.D. to 5000 A.D., those Accessions Commanders could get you the information you need. I think this would be a good topic for you to research further, Kai—especially when considering you plan to lead some of my teams back in time," Genesis slightly pushes himself from the table, signaling to Kai he wants to conclude the session.

Kai picks up on Genesis' nonverbal signal to conclude, "Okay, boss, I will look into these topics more.

It was a pleasure getting to speak with you again, Genesis."

"Thank you very much, Kai. It was a pleasure speaking with you too," Genesis smiles as he steps away.

Kai stacks his notes, gathering himself for the next phase in his research. He is eager for his upcoming mission. As he shuts off the light, his mind stirs—imagining the travels he may one day experience to the ancient lands casually discussed by the pilgrim. Perhaps, one day, he will be seated on the other side of this table.

5

Assessment of the 21st Century

"Greetings, Genesis."

"It is nice to meet with you again, Kai Aetos-Anthropos."

"Likewise, Genesis. Today we are scheduled to discuss your view of the 21st Century."

"Okay," Genesis concedes, "Currently I am working on my book which contrasts ancient Israel with 21st Century America—so it may be best to wait for my full assessment in that book."

"That would be an acceptable plan, Genesis. In the meantime today, would you like to offer us some brief insights into this topic? How did you see the 21st Century in your past life?"

Genesis pauses. He sighs—a partial, subdued sigh, indicating there is more air which wants to escape. The air within him seems caught between two opposing forces, one pushing and one pulling. In the inner struggle, his chest becomes motionless—resolving subconsciously to hold onto his breath as his mind attempts to jostle loose his thought. His face reddens. The pilgrim's shoulders stiffen and move upward—as if the chair is sliding up behind him. As his mind reemerges, Genesis' breathing pattern takes control of both his lungs and words—allowing for the synchronization of thought into punctuated thought bubbles . . .

"The 21st Century was an absolute mess: Being trapped within routines . . . Derision of the spiritual . . . Blindness to own problems while overly critical of others . . . Lack of compassion . . . Disposable plastic societies—ever intent on throwing away everything: People included. Fakeness at all levels—from the money as imaginary numbers all the way to the appearances of people. Disconnected zombies—addicted to dopamine manipulation via social media, computers, video games, and worst of all—cell phones, providing a means for people to be sucked into vanity at all times. Fake friends, fake relationships. People in the physical presence of other people, all glued to their own screen devices.

Society bereft of sense—rather than moving forward to grasp concepts of the 4th dimension, losing sight of the first three: length, width and height. Third-dimension humans preferring to yield a dimension in preference for the two dimensions of screens. Mass groups of three-dimension humans working diligently to become two-dimensional, as the Luminaries drifted ever further from their vision."

Kai reflected on the pain present in the words of the pilgrim. Each word picture appeared to strike within Genesis as it left his mind, as if being reluctantly torn from him as pages are torn from a book. Genesis appeared to be violating his own conscience by forcing himself to move beyond his natural limits. Out of compulsion it appeared, the pilgrim kept tearing more pages from within. . . . Another, then another.

The thoughts were so profound and organized—seeming as if Genesis were describing what he presently saw rather than distant memories. The pilgrim was clearly still connected to these past events—even though he was three millennia removed from them.

Kai was unsure what to say. Genesis' punctuated assessment and obvious personal connection dispelled the typically jovial jesting of Kai Aetos-Anthropos. Frankly, in his 5000 A.D. society, these concepts were foreign indeed. Kai settled on a phrase which he hoped would be perceived as adequately empathetic—as an attempt to appease the man for whom Kai had no understanding . . .

"Genesis, those people seem like a lost cause."

Genesis replies, "Not all were a lost cause. Some still had a yearning for something more—being drawn to the realization that there must be 'more to life.' This is why the faith of the Bible remained so compelling. It was the last remnant beckoning to people to walk by faith, not by sight."

With this, Genesis' frustrations were deep. He felt as if he brutishly tore the last pages from the book of his memories: The pages sticking to the binding—resisting the ripping, warning him to go no further. Nonetheless, he neglects himself—applying still more pressure, a most violent pressure, as the cover of the book collapses onto itself. Genesis holds within his mind this mangled book of his memories, brutalized by his lack of reverence in his last unrestrained moments. The pilgrim's mind is flooded with visions and emotions—each connected to his own perceived failures, through which he feels as if he completely forsook everyone and everything.

Genesis weeps.

Within himself, Genesis was struck by the candid assessment of Kai Aetos-Anthropos. Genesis realizes his harsh assessment of the 21st Century was perhaps inappropriate for the ears of Kai—making it seem as if Genesis perceived those ancient people as enemies. In truth, however, Genesis desired most of all to save them from the things which held them captive in the past. As he wept, Genesis' mind flooded with many conflicting thoughts.

As he wept, Genesis placed shame upon himself for breaking down in front of Kai—a person who he perceived could not understand. However, Genesis pushed himself beyond this temporary recoil—allowing himself to weep as he would if Kai were not present.

Genesis told himself he wanted Kai to see his pain. The pilgrim desired to unite humanity in concern for one another. In this quiet room, Genesis reasoned his tears may be the only way for Kai to truly see the pain experienced in the past. Genesis wanted Kai to see.

Often Genesis would weep to give his mind clarity—viewing his tears as the mind's attempt to reframe the impossible situations in which it found itself. When ancient humans could do nothing further to remove themselves from trouble, their own tears would form a mental fortress within themselves—giving them respite from the physical troubles around them. Thus, the pilgrim moves within his fortress, where he cycles through a series of inner switches. As a grand supercomputer, the mind of the pilgrim is rebooting as his subconscious and conscious balance themselves. The moat around the fortress rises and falls as the stronghold shifts to orient itself atop the physical circumstances in which the body finds itself. With his sobbing, Genesis opened a window in his fortress through which Kai could observe the futility felt by ancient humans.

The moment passes. Genesis gathers himself from within his stronghold and reemerges. This reemergence is signaled by the increasing displacement of jolts between each sob. Eventually the jolts halt as Genesis wipes his face with his sleeve.

Kai reattempts empathy by breaking the silence, "That must have been hard for you."

"It was, and still is."

"Wh-----"

"So many things seemed a lost cause. Feeling alone—as if I were the only one who could see things: Losing the ability to relate to people, abandoning them to themselves."

"Well you are with us now, and we want to listen to you." Kai felt as if he was beginning to understand.

Genesis passes his hand across his forehead and eyes, "I know, and I am thankful to be here with our people. I am working so hard to figure these things out because I don't want to see this happen again." He carefully plots the delivery of his words to hold back tears. With his final word, Genesis lowers his eyes below the brim of his hat. The dam breaks. He covers his face, receding in personal reflection once again. Genesis has learned to value such prompts to inner reflection. He hastens once again to his mental fortress as he hears the words of Kai echo near him, receding ever further in the distance . . .

"We are all listening now, Genesis. You are not alone anymore."

Genesis calls back through the wall of his consciousness before he closes the door of his mind. . . .

"Kai, we must find a way to rescue those who desire to be rescued. We must find a way to bring them to us."

Kai wonders at how quickly his heart has changed within the last minutes of this session. Before Genesis spoke, Kai had an enduring sense of security—feeling beyond all the ills which afflicted past humans. His advanced society had far removed him from the common pain experienced by his ancient ancestors.

Yet, now within this quiet room, the heart of Kai was transformed inwardly. The words of the pilgrim pierced deep within. For the first time, Kai Aetos-Anthropos considered the possibility of stepping outside his comfort for the sake of others.

As Genesis continued weeping, Kai was drawn to move to the other side of the table. He stood near the pilgrim—fearful to place his hand upon the visionary who jolted with sobs on the chair before him. Instead, Kai chose to remain silent, bowing his head in reflection. He did not understand how pain could abide within a man so deeply—causing pain three millennia later.

Genesis' sobbing was doing much more than mere words ever could. Within that room, Kai Aetos-Anthropos set aside himself. He chose to dedicate himself to the task of helping those for whom the pilgrim wept.

As Genesis wept, Kai's mind circled above and watched.

6

Advice for 3rd Dimension Humans

Genesis enters the room. Across the table, Kai's face is hovering above the papers before him. His neck is craned downward. He appears to be squinting, being evermore beckoned by the words on the page to move closer. Entranced by the siren song of the unknown writing, Kai Leon-Anthropos becomes oblivious to his surroundings within that inadequately lighted room. Who knows how long he has been there? Lately, Kai has been consumed with his study—diligently preparing himself with the knowledge he may need for his imminent mission into the past.

Genesis clears his throat—loudly.

Within his mind, Genesis thinks of the old movies where subtle cues, like coughing, were used to get people's attention. His mind wanders for a moment as he attempts to remember where he first saw this and why people do it. As was often the case with Genesis, his lack of memory led him to immediately drop the thought— abandoning it to a past which ever remains buried in the depths of his mind.

Kai—startled by the noise, looks up from his reading. The pilgrim across from him now stands silent and motionless with a walking cane in his hand. Kai at first assumed Genesis made the noise as a gesture of kind interruption. Now, after seeing the silence with which the pilgrim stands, Kai is unsure how to interpret the gesture. He considered the equal possibility that Genesis may either be jovial or he may be annoyed. In the silence of the room, Kai begins to think it is the latter.

"Sorry, boss," Kai offers to assuage what he interprets as annoyance.

Genesis reemerges from his subconscious, being jolted by the words of Kai, "Sorry for what?" Genesis' eyes once again survey the table ahead of him— recapturing the physical reality around him, item by item, until the complete picture reassembles in his mind.

Kai is patient—now realizing, perhaps, the pilgrim drifted for a moment to a faraway land. He gives him a moment to presumably reorient himself.

"It is good to see you again, Genesis." In an effort to gently guide the pilgrim back to the present, Kai offers further, "We are here today to discuss advice for 3rd dimension humans to become 4th dimensional."

Genesis is drawn into Kai's words and focuses upon them. He grasps the table ahead of him, supporting himself as he lowers his body into the chair. Now reoriented, Genesis is eager to discuss this topic. As a kind social gesture, Genesis motions to the stack of papers before Kai . . .

"It looks like you have been doing a bit of studying, Kai."

The jovial underestimation was laughable— considering Kai's voracious appetite for knowledge since he received his recommendation from his Accessions Commander. In fact, Kai's eyes were weary from reading—being ever pressed to seek further knowledge. He was inwardly driven by the thought that any of these documents may contain a secret bit of knowledge he needs to succeed in his mission.

Over the many days, Kai's studies had led him to the realization that he felt as if he knew nothing— absolutely nothing. This is the same realization which captures every visionary, being ever drawn further in the pursuit of knowledge: With every step further, the realization they had forgotten something deeper, a

87

prerequisite proverbial pebble—which upon further examination always turns out to be a mountain amidst and ever expanding range of mountains. Kai indeed was lost in this personal and professional quest: His mind ached, his eyes dry, his neck sore from craning and a permanent image of a paper sheet etched upon his closed eyes at the end of each day.

Kai responds, "Genesis, I . . ."

Kai is lost for words, unsure how to express his efforts in words. Should he offer a professional response—listing for his commander the specific topics he has researched? Surely, Kai considers, given his complete effort, it would not be fair for him to say anything in jest about his reading simply to gain a laugh from Genesis. Kai's studies have held within him a profound sense of gravity for the mission assigned to him. Kai has been brought to the realization of the responsibilities he will bear as a Team Leader. Every time he is drawn by his own physical limitations to set down a book, or to abandon pursuit of a seemingly insignificant pebble, Kai inwardly sees the faces of his team members. Then his mind swirls to the many people in society. His studies have led him to embrace the same weight held within the pilgrim—that all these people depend upon him. And he cannot fail them—no matter the constraints placed upon him by his own human limitations.

Kai's heart is heavy—very heavy. Somehow, Kai's heart begins to feel heavier—much heavier. His mind draws inward, catching on his heart—then it collapses within. Kai feels the room shift and cascade on him from all sides. The table and walls arch upwards and down, bearing down upon him . . . Heaviness bearing down upon him.

The walls each bear with them thoughts equally as heavy. Kai's mind flashes through thoughts of history—the many centuries of struggles leading up to the present . . . the suffering, the cruelty contained in those books. Things so forgotten—entire societies altogether lost, swallowed up by time.

Kai's mind raced through visions of the forsaken world. People who were buried in ground under rocks etched with words, each in grand ceremony. But in the many years hence, the rocks themselves yielding up the etched epitaphs before finally becoming consumed themselves by wind and water. Kai's mind raced through thoughts of each deceased human—with no remaining tribute to commemorate their contributions to history. Graves long abandoned, with the only remembrance being found within the minds of those students of history who happen upon the ghosts of the past.

Kai's mind was overwhelmed and broken by this crushing weight of futility afflicting endless generations of the forgotten. At once his mind desired to be free, yet he remained incapable of writhing out from under it.

Under this immense burden, Kai's mind now gave each thought an outward appearance—channeling each to the surface of Kai's body. Each told a tale of the transformation taking place within Kai's mind. Those unfamiliar with this burden may have missed the tensions present: Kai's loss of words, his changes in posture, his shift in appearance—eyes, mouth, skin. Yet, the pilgrim across from Kai was no ordinary man. Although socially awkward, it was this awkwardness which allowed Genesis to see people inwardly.

As Kai feels the heaviness building around him, Genesis allows Kai's tension to build inwardly. Being accustomed to grief, Genesis knows it must be allowed its course to benefit the human who holds it. Much as a weightlifter exposes his muscles to tension to promote growth, Genesis oversees Kai's present tension. Genesis allows the grief to build to the amount necessary to promote maximum growth within Kai. And, at that precise moment, Genesis allows the grief to move no further. He signals the halting of its advancement with the placement of his hand upon Kai's shoulder.

The pilgrim who had difficulty lowering himself in his chair a moment before, rejoins his hand across the room at the side of Kai. With the placement of the hand, Kai's mind breaks free of the weight. The walls recede—content now to resume their task of stretching the ceiling away from the floor.

Tears roll down Kai's face. His body jolts with each surge from his heart. The pilgrim stands next to Kai. Genesis knows that these tears will provide the energy Kai needs for the next phase of his studies. His tears will reset his mind—giving him the ability to approach a new set of mental challenges. Genesis often thought of tears in this way. A person cries as grief concludes a cycle. Those tears usher in the next cycle.

As Genesis stands silent, with his hand upon Kai's shoulder—being jostled with the sobbing, the pilgrim reflects within his mind upon John 3:5. He thinks about how those who will be saved will be born of water and the Spirit. Genesis reflects on the trauma of life—thinking about how the tears of those who suffer allow them to pass into new cycles of spiritual growth. He becomes sure of this for Kai. Genesis stands until Kai emerges ready to face his next phase of life.

"Thank you, Genesis."

Genesis smiles. At many times throughout his life, people have waited patiently for Genesis to regather himself from similar moments. Now it is his turn.

A moment passes. Kai—embarrassed to have broken down in front of his commander, now seems content to pretend as if the last moments never happened. Kai shifts the papers in front of him, noting water drops on some of the sheets. He slowly looks up, conscious that his appearance may now be marred as evidence of his sobbing.

Genesis is accustomed to seeing red eyes weary from weeping staring back at him. He is not judgmental—embracing such moments as evidence of a shared humanity. Indeed, he long desired for more people to be in such connection with their emotions. He viewed such moments as necessary events on the pathway to spiritual enlightenment.

Kai offers, "Genesis, thank you for meeting with me today. We have many readers, in the past as well as the present, who are 3rd dimensional. Could you explain how a 3rd dimension human becomes 4th dimensional?"

In the past, Genesis was considered a man *disabled*—one lacking the standard-issue abilities of the common man. Genesis' mind was indeed broken from many years on battlefields. Over the course of extended trauma, the pilgrim's brain was shattered in its attempt to somehow survive the un-survivable.

That word, *disabled*, still struck as a note of discord within the corridors of his mind. Although never spoken, he still heard its echoes as cruelly as when it was thrust upon him. In his old life, Genesis ever bore this word upon him. He was a man who was lost upon battlefields for his people . . . only to prepare himself to be utterly forsaken upon his return.

Genesis smirks—his mind being drawn to an irony extending three millennia. Genesis sits now as the sole survivor, at least for now anyways, of a distant, forgotten, ancient people. There were many people in his time—wiser, educated, being raised and protected as the pinnacles of society. Surely in his mind he mused they should be the ones sitting in this seat.

How indeed is the most disabled, barely surviving, mentally shattered, socially awkward pilgrim the one who is being asked about topics like multiple dimensions and time travel? The odds are astounding. He was a disabled nobody in his previous life—a person compelled by economy to fight the wars of the wealthy as they remained sheltered and safe.

Genesis looks at the young Kai across from him—enhanced with physical capabilities which would rival a lion or a tiger in his previous life. He matches gazes with Kai—taking note of physical features which would absolutely boggle the wisest men of the 21st Century. And in the midst of this setting, Genesis considers, *I am an ancient, disabled nobody, who no one cared about, yet now I have a lion-human asking me to explain the 4th dimension to people in 5000 A.D.*

Genesis' smirk transforms into laughter . . . A booming, laughter from the heart—carrying through the walls of the room: A laughter building for thousands of years. Mingled within his laughter, Genesis holds thoughts of sadness at the generations who were lost. Yet those dark tinges are rapidly overpowered by his intense feelings of vindication . . . new life . . . and salvation. *Finally!* Being lost for so many years, Genesis feels *found* in this moment—as now it is his turn to allow subdued tears to pass his guard.

This is the grandest discovery of himself. Perhaps the pilgrim has truly found a home. In this society, there are countless humans who are eager to listen and learn from this 21st Century outcast—a most glorious paradox in which Genesis is thankful to participate.

Genesis' laughter subsides. He passes his hand across his face, and begins, "Sorry, Kai. I guess this is an emotional time for all of us. But I think we are moving in opposite directions: You were saddened about the past you read about; and I am happy I somehow escaped it."

The irony strikes Kai, "That is interesting, Genesis. I guess we are moving in opposite directions . . . You moved forward in time; now I am seeking to go back."

Genesis and Kai experience a kinship extending through the table separating them. Genesis remembers the change of command ceremonies as outgoing and incoming military commanders would pass command authority to one another. These ceremonies involved the passing of a unit flag from one commander to another. In this moment, Genesis' mind passes to Kai's subconscious a flag just as tangible yet unperceived.

"Yes, you will, Kai. And one day you will be seated on this side of the table—perhaps explaining the 5th or even 6th dimension to a brave young human."

"Thank you, Genesis. I hope so. I will certainly give my best." The moment of Kai's breaking at the beginning of this session are now far away. His brief tears have already given way to a new cycle of hope which will carry him through the challenges of the following days— at least until he needs to cry again to reset the cycle.

"Okay, Kai, let's talk about the 3rd and 4th dimensions."

"Alright," Kai smacks with enthusiasm as he lightly smacks the table. In reverse motion, he sweeps up his pen and prepares to write.

Genesis speaks further, "Let's begin with an explanation of what it means to be a 3rd dimension human . . . To be 3rd dimensional means that the person is purely physical in their thinking—being mindful of only things with physical length, width, height. There are exceptions to this in the sense that those who are 3rd dimension humans can obviously grasp ideas, or mental images, but beyond this they are imprisoned within the 3rd dimension."

"What types of ideas or mental images can a 3rd dimension human grasp?"

"These will all be obvious—examples are things like 'time'—because 'time' does not consist of physical matter, nor does it have length, width, height. . . . At least time doesn't have any of those things from what we can see."

"Gotcha."

"A 3rd dimension human can obviously think about things—but for the 3rd dimension human 'thinking' is as close to the 4th dimension as they will ever get. So things like math, science and so on would be examples of things which can be thought about by 3rd dimension humans."

"But that is as far as they can journey from the 3rd dimension?"

"Yes, but by thinking one does not leave the 3rd dimension. They still remain within it. Actually, a great deal of damage can be done to society if people do not understand this. If for example, 'thinking' becomes the highest thing among a population of 3rd dimension people, then 'thinking' will begin to seem very profound and lofty. People will aspire to these thoughts as their highest goals. But ultimately these things among 3rd dimension people just become a grand echo chamber. No one is really breaking free from the 3rd dimension prison by their mathematics, physics or whatever. They are still firmly glued within those limits, but over time they begin to view their musings as something profound and enlightening. In reality, from our 4th dimension perspective, we would view even the most advanced 3rd dimension sciences as rats within a cage talking to the other rats about the bars of the cage. No one in the 3rd dimension gets beyond the bars—no matter how much they talk about the bars, or floor, or the other rats. So, as we understand from the 4th dimension—all the sciences of 3rd dimension humans 'at most' portray a partial, slight truth and 'at the least' they are simply rats talking to other rats about the bars of the cage within which they are imprisoned. Unless a 3rd dimension human comes to this realization, they will remain evermore trapped within the 3rd dimension. Period."

"Please tell me more."

"Okay. A good example would be the Luminary Systems. From the 4th dimension we can see what they really are. However, from the 3rd dimension, humans can only see the smallest part of each Luminary. So, everything a 3rd dimension human could observe and record about a specific Luminary would be an altogether

worthless assessment to a human with novice 4th
dimension vision. Indeed, it would at most be laughable—
especially when we consider that 21st Century humans
would often talk as if they had all the answers. Yet the
dimensional jumps are vast. I reckon that one day, when
5th dimension humans fill society, our 4th dimension
observations and recordings will seem akin to a
description of the bars from within a rat cage. Therefore,
no matter how enlightening 'thinking' may appear to a
society, it should be recognized that the pathway to
advancement will always be one which is first recognized
as 'spiritual.'"

"What do you mean?"

"Well, when humans do not understand something
about the natural world, they are inclined to ascribe it to
the 'spiritual'—thinking there must be an unseen reality
beyond the seen reality. This is what I mean by
'spiritual.'"

"Okay."

"So the pathway to human advancement will
always be spiritual. Always." Genesis shifts his speech to
pose a question, "In the past, many centuries before my
time, how did the ancient humans who were on the verge
of the 4th dimension view the 4th dimension?"

Kai answers, "As the realm of the supernatural."

"Exactly. So now, on the verge of us learning
about time travel and the 5th dimension, we view it as an
'unseen' reality beyond our seen reality. In truth, we do
not have words to adequately explain any of these

concepts, nor do we have the ability to teach someone step by step how to move from one dimension to the next. To do so, the individual human must embrace the 'unseen' reality beyond their vision. In this way, *all* advancements of humans will evermore be gained through spirituality—not by descriptions of the cage offered by the smartest rats."

"So what are the benefits of study and science within the cage?"

Genesis answers, "Of course there are benefits to science conducted within the rat cage—in other words, the science of 3rd dimension humans studying the 3rd dimension. In our analogy, it makes sense that smart rats would want to know everything about the food they are eating, the water they are drinking, the floor below them, the bars around them, and how their own bodies work. These are all useful to know within the rat cage itself. But, let's be candid: No rat is ever going to become free through 3rd dimension thinking or science. At most, maybe, the rats could find a way out of the cage through their 3rd dimension observations. But they never will advance beyond what they are if they study only what they are. The 3rd dimension rats could figure out how to live long and well, with purpose within the 3rd dimension. But to move beyond it requires what is defined as spiritual—finding and embracing the unseen."

"I like that, Genesis. To move forward, a person must see the unseen."

"Yes. In very ancient writing, this was called 'walking by faith, not by sight.' The major tragedy in my past life was that the 3rd dimension humans taught all the other 3rd dimension humans how to be most content within their 3rd dimension cage. They used the concept of 'outer space'—which now we know is ridiculous—to stretch their thinking of the 3rd dimension to infinite levels. And they would actually describe 'outer space' as infinite—a concept most absurd, yet effective in their purpose of completely distracting common people from the investigation of spiritual things. It worked—and for centuries we all became rats content with our cage. Eventually the bars disappeared as humans lost sight of their past understanding. Humans no longer thought in spiritual terms, so the 4th dimension was forsaken—in addition to all dimensions beyond that."

Kai guides the discussion, "Genesis, how can a 3rd dimension human become 4th dimensional?"

"Well, different 4th dimension humans can speak to their own experiences and how they became able to see the unseen. I can share with you my own experiences if you like."

"Yes, please."

"In some cases, people now learn to become 4th dimensional by learning from a teacher who has already mastered that vision. However, in my case, in now ancient society, I had no teacher. So my path began as a personal journey. I began reading the Bible. I liked it—especially its message of hope. The concept of God always being with me was captivating. So I kept reading. At my time, some people would brag about reading the entire Bible—it was a big, ancient book, mind you. But I absolutely devoured it. I kept reading it, over and over again. I taught it to other people, and began writing about it—examining its stories in extreme detail. I always ventured to understand for myself, so I made it a habit to write my own thoughts before I asked anyone their opinions. So, over many years, my connection to the Bible built as I became increasingly more mastered by it."

"You mean you mastered the Bible?"

"No, Kai. No one masters the Bible. Instead, a student of the Bible seeks to be mastered by it."

"I see. Kind of backwards, but I like it."

"It is an old saying," Genesis chuckles, "The Bible is indeed very special and was my guide in all things. I found I learned the most when I taught others. I began to hear many things inwardly as I spoke. I found also that when I prepared to teach other people, putting together notes, I would feel God teaching me first before I would teach other people. So, in this I began to sense I was a mediator, or a messenger—a channel through which God was speaking to people."

"Then you became 4th dimensional?"

"Not quite, but this was near the start. As I began to view myself as this channel, I began to view myself as really existing in two ways—responding to both the seen and unseen worlds. You should understand at this point, I was really struggling. It was after I served for many years in wars. So my grief was great. But, whereas you appear to be dealing with your grief in a healthy way, Kai, I developed the most terrible habit of suppressing my grief." Genesis subtly hints at Kai's grief expressed at the beginning of the interview. In this, Genesis makes a veiled attempt to encourage Kai to continue expressing his emotions in the future.

"How?"

"Well, instead of crying at times normal people should cry, I began in war to push down those emotions. Because I viewed myself as a strong man, I kept stopping myself from experiencing human emotions. But, as is the case which always happens, this habit of strong men eventually shattered my mind. In the aftermath of war, I discovered my inability to recapture those emotions I long held silent. My injuries made it even worse. So, ultimately these things led me to further pursue the teachings of the Bible. Whenever I experienced any difficulty coping with anything, I would bury myself in study—reading and writing, trying to figure it all out."

"Then you made the leap to the 4th dimension?"

"No, not yet. After this, I experienced more isolation. I began to understand things more clearly—especially the people in the Bible. When others would discuss the Bible, I began to feel anxious at most times—discontent with how these ancient people were often disrespected. So this led to still further isolation as I sought within the Bible vindication for the people within it who were kidnapped from within its pages. As I looked still further into the people in the Bible, I began to feel their experiences. Rather than looking down on them as ancient people, I began to look at them as people akin to myself. Just as I was broken by war, and was currently broken and isolated in its aftermath, so these people in the Bible were also broken by tragedy."

"So, when you were feeling isolated, you began to feel the things they felt."

"Yes. And within this is the key—in my experience. The pathway to the 4th dimension is through a break from your 3rd dimension self. For me, it started after my first war experience. In the aftermath, my wife gave me an audio-Bible."

"A what?"

"An audio-Bible is a recording of the Bible. Throughout each day, I developed the habit of listening to the Bible all day long. I ended up flooding my mind with the same thoughts which guided the ancient prophets. During those years of my life, I was at a very low point— having so much trauma in my past afflicting my mind, and being unsure how to cope with any of it. So, another habit I developed was Bible memorization."

"What did you do for that?" Kai asks.

"I began memorizing entire chapters of the Bible—specifically John chapters 1-6. When walking each day, I would silently recite these chapters to myself. I did this so often that over time my mind shifted in its operation."

"Shifted?"

"Kai, my mind started working more like a recorder or a tape player. My thoughts of the supernatural began to be akin to me pressing 'play' on a device and me passively listening to my own thoughts run their course within my mind. Within my mind I no longer directed thoughts—but rather I set processes in motion, like beginning to silently quote John, and then the script continued in my mind uninterrupted."

"Okay," Kai thinks he understands, but is still not sure what it means to be passive within one's own mind.

Genesis perceives Kai's thoughts and addresses them: "Kai, a person can control their mind directly or indirectly. It is common for those who are stuck in trauma to develop the ability to separate from themselves within their own mind. This allows the person to remain physically within a tough situation, while their mind draws further 'out' from it. This is textbook '4th dimension'—the ability to move 'in/out' to see 3rd dimension things in their fullness."

"So, then you became 4th dimensional?"

"Well, things had to get much worse first. My mind was capable of playing recordings as I remained passive within, yet outside the process. Then, I went back to war two more times."

"Wow."

"Yes. In these later deployments, I felt very isolated. I was a team leader in the U.S. Marines and had no one to whom I could look for guidance. I was stuck for years—ever being compelled to maintain myself for the sake of the men who depended upon me. My isolation grew. To make matters worse, I experienced a head injury—which completely changed my brain. So, within myself, I developed the ability—quite unknowingly, to separate myself from myself. I became shattered."

"So, then you were 4th dimensional."

"No," Genesis' frustration matches Kai as he reflects on these lost memories and the futility which once consumed his mind. "Kai, it was a process that dragged on. It was so painful. In the many years after my survival, I struggled. I had such a difficult time, I often thought I was destined to have died in some foreign land at a certain time, but somehow I missed my appointed time. I began to view myself as a ghost—still existing yet somehow altogether forgotten. My relationships with other humans fragmented in the aftermath—leading me further into the path of isolation. Their painful withdrawals from me further convinced me of my wraith-like existence: I should have died earlier, but since I missed my time I was forsaken to suffering."

"I'm so sorry, Genesis," Kai desires to grab the pilgrim's hand from the table to hold it in his own. Kai feels for this man who had to endure such pain. Yet, as was always the case for Genesis, the intimidation of his form compelled Kai to retreat from this act of courageous compassion. Genesis often desired to have people to show him common human expressions of concern—but his power, force and physical form formed an impressive barrier which warded off even the most brave. Thus, the pilgrim was so powerful in his previous life and the present that he altogether ceased to be human in the sight of others.

(Note: *Perhaps indeed it was this intimidation warding which enabled Genesis to attain the 4th dimension. He was left alone for many years—which allowed his grief to complete its full, good process. Whereas other men were constantly deterred from grief by people who attempted to heal them or dissuade them from grief with comparisons; the pilgrim remained immersed within it firmly—becoming fully aware of every aspect of the common stirrings which occurred within his own mind. This full experience of grief provided the ground upon which Genesis' spirit could grow— eventually breaking free from the soil from which it first emerged.*

Thus, when people are afflicted in grief, others should not attempt to constantly remove the rich soil. They should not seek to constantly weed the garden of the one who suffers. Let it all grow—weeds and all. Do not trample upon any of it, or encroach upon its boundaries.

Bear with those who suffer in silence, as the person's spirit learns to carefully navigate through the darkness with God's help. Allow their mind to learn to communicate with their own spirit. Eventually, with your silent support, the one who suffers can begin to see through the weeds around them. Then God Himself will direct them to carefully tend the garden from within, gently approaching each plant with profound reverence—

choosing for themselves how their new garden will be appear. Finally, the Good Shepherd serves as the Gate to lead the person out when the time is right.

Grief is not a disease to be healed; it is a pathway. It helps the person escape from the 3rd dimension. Upon attaining full growth in the midst of a garden of grief, the one who suffers can become remarkably powerful—a supernatural visionary in the midst of a society where people constantly run away from suffering. Notwithstanding, I digress . . .)

Also, in the past, Genesis' default ability to intimidate others by sheer presence doubtlessly saved his life many times—deterring potential enemies from targeting his team. Thus, Genesis' ability to intimidate would make his team appear unassailable—or at least perceived as not worth provoking due to the stinging counter which his enemies reasoned would melt the earth around them. Through his ability to intimidate, the pilgrim would win would-be battles through this ethereal manipulation of any would-be attacker.

Although he was physically broken, retaining only a fraction of his past physical prowess, it was this hidden, ethereal power which now intimidated humans in 5000 A.D. Frankly, they did not comprehend the deep spirituality of the pilgrim. Therefore humans tended to restrain themselves in his presence.

Nevertheless, Genesis was human, or at least still partly so. In fact, Genesis now felt his heartbeat—forming shock waves, passing warmth and surges across his vision. The surges echoed through his body, being visible in the quaking of his hands below his face. Genesis' dismisses the thought of compassion extended to him. His mind is still raw from the constant rejection which afflicted him in his past life.

Genesis considers anew the possibility . . . no, *the reality*, although he is similar to other men, he was not like other men—he is something different. . . .

Genesis hears Kai's thought and his desire to grab his hand. Yet the pilgrim gently dissuades the young man inwardly, swaying him from his thought.

"Thank you, Kai. It means a lot to hear you say that," Genesis smiles. "Well, as I struggled with the aftermath of war, and my increasing isolation from others, I went still further within myself. I spoke to counselors about my experiences, but eventually I arrived at a dead end."

"What do you mean?"

"I reached a point where my counselors would begin to cry with me. They had nothing to say to coach me from the 3rd dimension bars within my mind. So, as I explained in detail the common thoughts which afflicted me hourly, counselors would begin crying. My testimony would often break them—at times they would cry even when I would not. I received a clear vision: My mere presence melted those around me. As wax before a fire, my words dissolved people. They just could not bear it. They could not bear any of it."

"Why?"

"Somehow I think my words began to strike at the heart of their own experiences. When I would speak their minds would draw them powerfully to their own past experiences—making them raw within their minds. I think this is what happened. In some cases it might have been that they were moved out of pure sympathy for me, but I am not sure. I guess it doesn't really matter anymore," Genesis retreats from the thought. "But when my counselors started to break before me, it made me feel good in the moment—the prospect of receiving such concern from a gentle human. However, in the aftermath it led me further into a path of isolation: Even the best minds—people who prepared their entire life to help me, could find nothing to say to assuage my condition. Any attempt to heal through 3rd dimension thinking was absolutely futile—and acknowledged to be so by all my counselors. For me, the 3rd dimension became an absolute dead end. I was alone."

Kai chases a red herring: "Were the counselors wrong to cry?"

"No, Kai. Humans should never halt their emotions. Once a person gets into a habit of silencing their conscience, eventually their conscience stops speaking to them. In a way it was very helpful for me to see counselors cry because it encouraged me to reembrace for myself this ability which I previously restrained within myself," Genesis summarizes, "When people are prompted to cry, they should cry."

"Got it."

"However, this example highlights the futility of my situation. I learned firsthand there are things which happen to humans where there is no help to lift them from their condition. Think of loss. A person who loses a long-time friend or family member will *always* have that grief present. Kai, it never goes away. There is nothing that can be said or taught to convince the mind of a person to completely forsake that grief. It's always there," Genesis pauses, then elaborates, "In truth, we would not want to wish away our grief anyway. To do so would be to forget the one we lost. Surely, in this we find the human condition: Being human in this fallen world means learning to live with unresolvable grief. But, that grief can give rise to a higher, 4th dimension existence. . . . Maybe that is the whole point. Grief helps us to find our way out."

"I see," Kai is unfamiliar with this type of grief, but he is doing his best to learn.

"Well, moving forward in my experience, I had to break free from the 3rd dimension prison around me. When I suffered in the 21st Century, it was common for people to always offer comparisons. They would say things like, 'This other guy has it worse than you.' No matter how grave the condition through which one was suffering, 3rd dimensional humans around them would ever seek to highjack them from their grief and self-discovery. Now, however, we know the path to the 4th dimension is through trauma. In fact, there is no such thing as faith without trauma as a prerequisite. It just cannot exist."

"I remember you explaining this in your David book."

"Yes. But, this habit of people using comparisons in a bizarre attempt to motivate those who were suffering was most hurtful—completely derailing the spiritual emergence of those who suffered. In the 21st Century, it was never okay for a person to simply have grief and learn from it. Those around them, being imprisoned in the 3rd dimension, would cast thoughts upon those afflicted with pain."

"Example?"

"Kai, you will not like any of this stuff. It is very evil—the height of 3rd dimension cruelty."

Kai came far in his quest for enlightenment. Although he arrived at this treacherous climb in his journey, being warned by the pilgrim to go no further, Kai chose to press forward . . .

"Please tell me, Genesis."

Genesis, being content at abandoning his explanation with a general reference, conceded to give Kai raw examples of 3rd dimension cruelty. . . .

"Kai, the examples are without limit. When someone lost a child, there would be others who would say, '*Well at least you didn't lose your husband because that is worse.*' In any case where a person suffered, there would always be people who compared their suffering to others who they thought had it worse. The government would even turn those who suffer into propaganda to shame those who they determined to be 'suffering less'— I guess in an ill attempt to motivate them through pure negativity. The government and veteran agencies would create advertisements with veterans who were missing arms and legs, or who suffered devastating burns. At first, when considering these things, it seemed a noble venture—the government and charitable organizations trying to uplift an injured individual. However, the 3rd dimension reality was apparent when viewing it from outside. These organizations were exploiting these warriors for personal gain—either to increase organization donations or to coerce specific actions from those likewise disabled through negative reinforcement. The 3rd dimension message in these was always the same: *Here is a man who is missing this, if you are missing anything less, stop complaining.* Thus, the 3rd dimension rats did their best to deter all people from their *own* journey through *their* grief. They exploited those who suffered to the uttermost—robbing them of the most precious achievement by distracting them from the road of grief which leads to 4th dimension enlightenment. The 3rd dimension rat cage had a way of turning those who suffered into social outcasts—who were never permitted to simply feel their own experiences for themselves. The 3rd dimension system re-victimized and violated those who suffered. This was a most grievous evil. It was rampant and those who did not suffer absolutely reveled in the power they presumed upon themselves—wielding the ability to determine the validity of suffering endured by others," Genesis summarizes, "It was one thing to suffer. But the truly unbearable suffering occurred in the re-victimization which humans routinely afflicted upon one another with their comparisons. They treated grief as if it were something that needed to be immediately dispelled or cured. When, in reality, abiding within grief and slowly moving through it is the only way in which a person can advance themselves. Grief is not a disease; it is a pathway."

Kai was speechless.

Genesis continued, "This was the terror of the 21st Century. We were rats in a 3rd dimension cage—all of us. The rats who were in power did everything they could to keep us in the cage. Whenever a person suffered, giving them occasion to look to the unseen in their journey of self-discovery, the head rats would always shout out, *'Think instead of these bars! Think instead of these other rats!'* So their propaganda—along with all the other comparison nonsense, served its 3rd dimension purpose: *Keep the rats within the cage. At all costs: Keep the rats within the cage,*" Genesis punctuates in his delivery, offering his spiritual assessment of the cruelty of the rats in the cage, *'Do not allow them to think about spiritual things. Do not let them escape.*"

"Why did they do that?" Kai is confused and aghast at the cruelty of now ancient humans.

"Who knows? I am sure some had no idea what they were doing was wrong. The 3rd dimension has a way of sweeping people up when there are no 4th dimension visionaries to challenge the evils within. Of course, to a 3rd dimension human, what I say seems most critical and rude—describing the fallen Earth as a rat cage. However, this is the true reality of those who were trapped within the system of the 3rd dimension Earth. Those who have escaped the bars of the cage can see this clearly—crystal clear. So, attempting to communicate this reality is most frustrating. Seeing something so clearly, yet altogether outside the perception of others. Thus, the visionary is often rejected as a maniac."

"What if a person accidently fell into these patterns of behavior?"

"In cases where a person unwittingly fell into these patterns, they need to simply change their behavior. Allow people to process grief. Don't dismiss or judge their grief. The only path to the 4th dimension is through grief. We understand this now. When someone is on the pathway to self-discovery, do not hinder them from their enlightenment with comparisons. Let them suffer, grieve and become fully human. Humans are intended to be 4th dimensional. Do not hinder their spirituality," Genesis steers his thought inward, "In my personal journey to 4th dimension capability, I was at first hindered by such comparisons. So I started separating myself from such 3rd dimension distractors. At the time I did not understand the bigger 4th dimension picture. I simply knew it did not feel good being trashed and measured all the time by people who truly did not understand my grief. Although I became even more isolated, I was able to finally break free from false 3rd dimension thinking. I began to grow in my understanding of the physical reality around me. Then I gained perception—I began to see the rats within the cage. Then I could feel the floor and the bars of the cage around me. I experienced a complete disconnection with those determined to remain within—who were intent on maintaining their power by holding captive an economic pyramid beneath them. I saw the world around me as entirely fake. Even the money we used was fake, being based on absolutely nothing—not gold, not silver, just paper, and often just existing as imaginary numbers in bank accounts. Thus, was the height and glory of the 3rd dimension—people filling themselves to the brim with something that was truly worthless and altogether imaginary, ever in pursuit of more imaginary numbers."

"Thank you for explaining, Genesis."

Genesis smiles. The pilgrim explains further, "For me, moving from 3rd dimension to 4th dimension thinking was a spiritual process. I began to understand people, and as I reflected on their suffering, I felt from within their bodies what they felt."

"How?"

"Well, in my first book on the ancient warrior-king, David, I discuss this in detail."

"I read it, but I think I need to go back and re-read it," Kai says with a mixture of excitement, yet overwhelming dread at the prospect of increasing his mental workload. He feels if he reads any more books, he will himself turn into a book.

"I can explain it. I know your workload is already heavy enough."

Kai smiles. He appreciates the gesture from Genesis.

Genesis continues, "In my book on David, I provide my notes surrounding the letters we sent back to him. When reading everything about David in the Bible, it becomes clear he was a man deeply wounded by trauma and warfare. Ultimately, in his prayers, we see David becomes capable of seeing God as a fortress of protection which travelled with him. David also becomes capable of experiencing events from within the bodies of future people—most notably, David writes about the actual experiences of the Lord Jesus."

"So you are saying David actually experienced events from within the body of the Lord Jesus?"

"Yes. The people of the Bible were not ordinary people. They were not shackled by the restraints of the 3rd dimension. People like David in the Bible were not writing poetically or using figures of speech about future events. Nor were they recording their own thoughts and imaginations. Rather, people like David, were able to move 'out' of the 3rd dimension to the 4th dimension, where they could experience events separate from themselves."

"How?"

"From a 3rd dimension perspective, David was able to separate from his own body as a symptom of a psychological dysfunction in his brain. The brain dysfunction was called PTSD, or post-traumatic stress disorder, and the symptoms which caused his ability to experience 'out of body' events were called 'depersonalization' and 'derealization.' In other words, David experienced so many bad things that his brain developed the ability to separate from itself mentally—allowing him to be transported to events outside himself," Genesis pauses—looking at the puzzled Kai across from him. Then Genesis offers, "Smart rats in the 3rd dimension cage of the 21st Century told us other rats about how our brains work."

"So, David imagined it?"

"No, he was transported to future events—similar to how we use the 4th dimension, and presumably how I used the 5th dimension. But it appears what happened to me was permanent—hence why I am still here."

Kai quips, "So, David was 4th dimensional? When exactly did he live?"

"Surprising, right? This is exactly what I thought when I arrived at this realization. To answer your question, David lived around 1000 B.C."

"1000 A.D.?"

"No, B.C."

"What? What's that?"

"B.C. means 'before Christ.' Apparently your studies having carried you back too far, Kai," Genesis chuckles.

Kai is stuck, "So, Genesis, you mean David was a 4th dimension human who lived six-thousand years ago!?"

"Yes. He might have achieved some hybrid between the 4th and 5th dimensions—because he routinely described events which occurred one-thousand years later."

"Absolutely remarkable."

"It is truly amazing, Kai. Of course David's ability was not from a 3rd dimension brain dysfunction, but the dysfunction contributed in some way to his development of ability. In the Bible, this ability to speak about future events was called 'prophecy.' Although not necessarily all people who called themselves prophets were actually 4th or 5th dimensional. Some just gave people inspiration. But the ones who wrote in the Bible would actually see things in the future through the use of these higher dimensions," Genesis is caught up in the rapturous discussion—seeing in Kai's eyes the same gleam which captured his own mind at these realizations thousands of years earlier. Genesis repeats Kai's reflection, "Kai, it is as you said—absolutely remarkable. In that time, we would call it 'miraculous.' Prophets were indeed very powerful and mysterious."

"What were the prophets like? Were they super-humans?"

Genesis looks at Kai before him. He is struck at the irony of Kai's question. The enhanced human is attempting to establish common ground with ancient biblical prophets—filled with wonder at the possibility they might be similar in form to himself.

"Kai, the prophets were completely ordinary in the 3rd dimension. They had no characteristics or special physical abilities—apart from what was common to the humans at their time. Although David was agile, strong and proficient as a warrior—physically he would not have been akin to your prowess. However, what made prophets different was the presence of God within them."

"You mean, *the* God?"

"Yes—the prophets in the Bible were said to have the Spirit of God abiding with them. It is the same Presence later poured out on all who follow Christ. So, the 4th or even 5th dimension capabilities of David were something which was made available to all followers of the Bible," Genesis pauses, then continues, "This is why it is so sad to think about what was lost during my lifetime. People walked away from a spiritual power which is still mysterious to us six-thousand years after David's life. The people of my time preferred a 3rd dimension rat cage to the wonders of what was taught in the past. It is most unfortunate and heartbreaking to consider what happened."

"What happened?"

"Well at the time of the prophets in the Bible, they went by different names and their missions spanned many generations. Most were killed off by those intent on stifling true spiritual progress. This continued for many generations—and the Bible is a testimony of those times. Then, around the time in which I lived previously, everything spiritual was re-labelled."

"Re-labelled?"

"To simplify, 3rd dimension people continued to teach 3rd dimension things, but they high-jacked all institutions which previously taught people to walk by faith, not by sight. In the teaching of the 3rd dimension rats, the bars of the rat cage continued to grow wider and wider—until humans began to see the bars themselves as being infinitely wide, stretching in all directions of the 3rd dimension. This was done so all people could see any more was the three-dimensions. This continued unchecked until people began to revere and honor the very specks of light on the bars of the rat cage— supposing each dot of light was really an unimaginably large glowing juggernaut made of celestial gas. And, like the juggernauts of old, these 3rd dimension falsehoods were used to roll and crush human spirits—forever dooming them to the 3rd dimension. People became incapable of seeing anything outside the 3rd dimension because it was taught the 3rd dimension was infinite," Genesis shifts, "Spiritual teaching once beckoned 3rd dimensional people to embrace the spiritual, higher dimensions as the prophets of old. Yet around the 21st Century, 3rd dimension thinking took over spiritual teaching as well. The 3rd dimension teaching became

119

increasingly focused on keeping people content with the rat cage around them. Preachers and teachers, whose positions were once occupied by those on the verge of being 4th dimensional, now had their positions filled by people bereft of true spirituality. They preached messages which were focused only on physical things—with only veiled references to anything beyond," Genesis' voice becomes heavy as he trails his last words, "They forgot. The words—written in the Book, vanished from the pages. People could read, but the words became entirely veiled to them. Preachers would speak of God as if He were present in a far off 3rd dimension galaxy . . . just totally incapable of imagining anything outside the three-dimensions—to the point of even consigning God to His own rat cage within their minds. Spirituality was lost. It was swallowed up by the bars of the rat cage. No one could see anything further."

"Sorry, Genesis," Kai is not sure what to say. The concepts spoken by Genesis are so foreign to him. Kai's mind races with questions—still reeling at the thought of 5th dimension humans who lived before the spiritual collapse. For Kai, it was a tragedy most severe to have such ancient visionaries drowned out by the centuries after them.

Genesis beckons Kai away from his reflection, "We will figure it out, though." The pilgrim speaks hopefully and assertively. As a warrior, Genesis learned to always project confidence to his troops. Today, although dealing with these raw topics, Genesis is reminded he must maintain that assertive confidence before Kai. After all, Kai will need to have memories of his commander's unshakable gusto to motivate him when he is alone with the faces of his own troops pasted to him in watchful expectation. Genesis truly has no idea how these problems will be resolved—he is often conflicted with these thoughts. However, before Kai, the pilgrim smacks the table and repeats—as if to convince Kai outwardly, and also himself, "We will figure this out!"

Kai responds instantly, as if echoing in cadence— jostled by the shaking table and the sound ringing like a pop of gunfire, "We will figure it out, boss!"

Kai is momentarily distracted from his reeling mind before it again speaks to him, urging him to ask more questions. His mind sticks on a point, realizing something grand, as if he received a revelation of the larger picture . . .

"So the letters to David in your book? . . ."

Genesis smiles and leans back in his chair. Although Kai knew, he never connected the dots for himself. He never understood the mind driving the Accessions Command. Now, after hearing for himself the process which led to Genesis' awakening, he is startled at the realization of the alarming ambition of the pilgrim seated before him.

Kai considered the prospect of reaching David: It is a grand goal, but how far back could they reach? Kai never met a Marine before, but he was learning to never underestimate the pilgrim before him—and the grandeur of expectation held within a Marine's mind. If anyone could do it, Kai was certain the pilgrim could find a way.

The room settles as Kai continues, "So, how did you become 4th dimensional?"

"Similar to David: Trauma survival, then depersonalization and derealization. It became natural to dwell in the disconnections of my mind. As I moved onto the Luminary Watchhand—which at the time I had no idea what it was, mind you, no one taught me anything—I somehow felt as if I were 'shifting' forward. It is hard, if not impossible to explain, but the 'shift' caused me to see a cascade of Luminary Systems—which at the time I had no idea what they were. I then emerged within this one in present year. After finding myself in this place, it was not until later that I learned the official names of the Luminary Watchhand and the Luminary Systems. So, although I was able to do what no one else could, I still had to learn many things from scratch in this Luminary System. So for me, achievement of 4th dimension and 5th dimension capabilities occurred at the same time," Genesis pauses to make sure Kai is still with him. Then he continues, "Not all 4th dimension humans are the same in their abilities, however. For example, when one starts things are unclear—seeming as lights passing beyond one's closed eyes or static. Yet with time, and practice, the 4th dimension abilities gain clarity—with the person becoming capable of an unseen ability akin to depersonalization. It is the best way I can explain it."

"I see."

"Then once a human is 4th dimensional, they vary in ability—most notably seen from the Luminary Watchhand. In order to travel from one Luminary System to another, novice 4th dimension humans need to move at the peak of a Luminary retrograde, as viewed from their present position. This allows them to 'aim,' as it were, at a stationary target. If they cannot move, they will not be able to move onto the Luminary Watchhand, no matter how much they try. In other words, it is not like someone can aim, miss and fall off into the Outer Darkness. If a person cannot 'jump,' then they won't be able to move," Genesis checks for acceptance, "Does that make sense?"

"It does," Kai answers.

"Another way to put it: Either the bridge is there or it isn't. The Luminary Watchhand is like an ethereal bridge. Once you are on it, you will make it to the place on the other side where you are aimed. There is no such thing as the bridge falling apart from under the person, or the bridge swinging off target. So the problem is more with a matter of perception. A novice 4th dimension human's problem is that it is difficult for them to see the Luminary Watchhand bridge, except for specific times where it seems most logical to them. When there is a pause in a Luminary System retrograde as it reverses movement, it is then that the novice 4th dimension human is most capable of movement—because it makes the most sense to do so then . . . Point A to Point B," Genesis smiles now. He is glad he continued—being more confident of his second explanation than his first.

"Perfect, thank you," Kai agrees with Genesis' subtle self-assessment. The second explanation lands well with Kai. "So, how does a more advanced 4th dimension human differ from a novice?"

"Well, novices run into problems due to their retrograde limitation."

"What do you mean?"

"Not every Luminary System has visible retrogrades. So, if a novice 4th dimension human is moving from one Luminary System to another, they could reach a Dead End. Or they could reach a Luminary System where the next retrograde is not visible for a very long time. If this happens they will be stuck within that Luminary System."

Kai clarifies, "The novice will be able to make it within the three-dimensions of the Luminary System, but once they are on the ground they will not be able to find another Luminary System to jump to?"

"Exactly. This is why it is important to never travel like this. There are many uncharted Luminary Systems which still remain unexplored. If a person were to find themselves at an uncharted Dead End, who knows how long they would be stuck there."

"In other words, pack a lunch," Kai jests.

"Yeah," Genesis shrugs, "Better not to try it at all. A person should stick to the charts and take a team with them. That's my advice. Even now, I do not do things solo. It is always wise to take a person with you—a 'battle buddy' as we used to call them. Usually whenever I venture out I always like to have a good navigator who can track details for me. Although I do well in some things, my memory most times is very bad." Genesis uses this as a good opportunity to use himself as an example to promote responsibility. He knows people listen to his words—so he considers it likely if he speaks out against travelling alone it may deter people from doing it. Genesis has a knack for always considering the secondary effects of his words and actions. "But to answer your question, Kai, an advanced 4th dimension human can use the Luminary Watchhand at will. They do not need a retrograde. They can simply see it and jump between Luminary Systems at will. An advanced 4th dimension human can also escort others who are physically within their heart's electrical field. We have done different experiments. We found if one is travelling with an advanced 4th dimension human, they merely need to be touching each other—like holding hands."

"Alright, I know I have kept you here probably beyond our schedule, but I have one more question. It is sort of a theoretical one."

"Oh boy," the pilgrim quips. Genesis is eager to answer questions and time is no factor now, but he cannot resist the temptation to give Kai a hard time.

"Yeah, here goes: previously you discussed the possibility of further dimensions beyond the 4th dimension. Although not yet gaining official recognition, do you have any further thoughts on dimensions beyond?"

"Yes. I love this topic! Like I said earlier, the path to human advancement will *always* be spiritual. Always. By nature, to see more than we can see requires we see the 'unseen.' So to the 3rd dimension human, the 4th dimension will seem something unseen and beyond their physical perception. The same applies to the 4th dimension human and their thoughts of the 5th dimension. Although unconfirmed, I think there are many dimensions beyond the 5th dimension—leading all the way to the footstool of God the Father. . . . So, how does this apply? Recently we have been developing procedures for Wanderers," Genesis pauses, thinking it possible Kai may not be familiar with the term. "Have you heard about Wanderers, Kai?"

"No, but you definitely piqued my interest! Please tell me."

"Okay. Wanderers are humans who we find in dimensional travel. Often these humans have no idea where they are, or how they arrived there. It is very puzzling. However, the teams we send out have specific instructions on procedures for Wanderer encounters."

"I heard of this, but I never really understood it, Genesis," Kai reflects.

"Well, think about it this way: In the 21st Century, I achieved 4th dimension capability—and even 5th dimension, which allowed me to come here. Yet, let's imagine I never made it here. Who knows where I would have went to? Eventually I would have needed someone to explain what was happening when I was found. I guess you could think of my discovery as my own Wanderer experience here—even though I figured it out before someone had to find me."

"I see."

"So, when thinking about my experience, it really is not even remarkable. In fact, as we discussed earlier, we have Bible prophets like David who did far greater, many millennia before my earlier life. I reckon it is possible, we may happen across Wanderers in our journeys from faraway times, similar to people from the Bible."

"Interesting."

"Yes, but my thoughts on this topic go further. I really want to figure this out, Kai . . ." Genesis trails off in anticipation.

Kai cannot help leaning forward. He peers at Genesis, leaning close as if he is going to hear a secret whispered across the table.

Genesis perceives Kai's excitement and notes his slight lean forward in anticipation. Genesis has always had an ability for theatrical performance in his speech delivery before troops. It was a part of his ability to inspire and motivate. Genesis keys in on this opportunity in a predictable and memorable way. He mirrors Kai's gesture, leaning forward himself. Genesis raises his hand above the table—beckoning Kai to inch closer, although the table remains a barrier. To heighten the moment, Genesis places his hand aside his face and lightly whispers as he dartingly glances over his shoulders—

pretending as if he must conceal his words from secret listeners who seek to snatch them from his breath . . .

"There are 7th, 8th, 9th dimension people out there. There has to be," Genesis adds, "Kai, I'm messed up. My mind is not right at all. My memory is bad—and I often forget where I am. Sometimes my balance is so bad I can barely stand. I really have a tough time lining up with people in conversation. I feel as if I was struck by a giant hammer which knocked my soul out of my body. I'm here, but I am so detached from my body. Kai, I am an absolute mess inside," Genesis pauses, then summarizes, "People used to tell me I was disabled."

"Really?"

"Yes, but Kai, I did 5th dimension time travel! I was a *disabled* person who did something that no one else can do—even now. Three millennia later still no one can do what a *disabled*, broken person did—without anyone to teach him. Do you get the implication here?"

Kai thinks he does, but leans in closer for Genesis to finish painting this picture with his words.

"Kai, I knew tons of people with disabilities far beyond my own. It was common, Kai. We even had multiple generations afflicted with disorders—with many children being born or developing these problems. And, some, from a 3rd dimension perspective were very bad—being totally incapacitated. In my time, society just wrote people off. Anyone who wasn't determined to be 'normal' was just put aside and dismissed. But Kai, I know they are out here—somewhere. These children and adults:

Thousands of them. We just can't see them yet. In my heart, I know those children are all here—probably doing things we cannot fathom, maybe even in the 10th dimension."

Kai nods, grasping at the words of the pilgrim. He struggles with the concept of such deep suffering experienced by many people in the past—even though he has never seen such a thing. He is convinced in a moment by the pilgrim.

"Kai, our path forward as humans will rely on these people who were forsaken by the past. They have grand things to teach us. And we will be the people who find them. We will bring them here."

7

Discussion of the 1st-6th Dimensions

"Hello, Genesis."

"Hello, Kai Anthropos-Anthropos. It is my pleasure to see you."

"Likewise, Genesis." Kai smiles—eager for their planned topic of discussion. He arrives with a longing—being content, and desiring above all to let the pilgrim speak. Kai wants to listen. He wants to understand. . . .

"Genesis, today we are scheduled to discuss dimensions. I plan to remain quiet as I take notes. Unless you have prerequisite matters you would like to discuss, please feel free to begin with an explanation of the 1st dimension moving forward to your theories concerning the 6th. I have been looking forward to this discussion for a very long time, and I do not want to become a distraction. So, if you approve, I would like to remain quiet and listen to your uninterrupted teaching," Kai concludes by asking the pilgrim for his acceptance, "Agreed?"

Genesis nods.

The eagerness of Kai is matched by the man across from him. Genesis is ever enthusiastic when approaching this topic. There is so much depth—just layers of wonderful mystery when reflecting on the majesty with which God constructed the created order. The pilgrim feels honored, yet inadequate to unpack this wisdom for his listeners and readers—whom he knows will doubtlessly move with intention over his words many times, ever searching . . . ever gleaning from among them truths to help them on their own journeys.

Above all, Genesis views himself as a fellow traveler in the process—a man simply sharing what he knows. And within this identity is security. He is not claiming to be an expert. Rather, he is a man simply sharing what he knows and has seen. In the habit of old, Genesis lights the torch within his mind, preparing to run his course before passing the fire to each of his readers. What they decide to do with his wisdom will become a journey owned only by themselves. Thus, the pilgrim begins speaking . . .

"Thank you, Kai. I share your enthusiasm, so I hope I can do an adequate job in my explanations." Genesis smiles at Kai across from him. A gesture matched in kind by the young man and embellished as Kai motions courteously with his hand for Genesis to continue.

Genesis presses forward, beginning with this word a journey which will declare the layers of creation—from its foundational aspects to the limitations of the pilgrim's vision. What has taken him a lifetime of discovery to build, he now yields freely to those who are thirsty for knowledge . . .

"Dimensions are best described as layers of the created order established by God. In my thinking, based on the ancient Bible, the dimensions are part of the divine plan to bring creation back to perfection. So it is not that things were made into dimensions just for the sake of God complicating things. Rather, after the created order was corrupted by the fall of Lucifer, God allowed creation itself to become fragmented. This makes it where the created order can return to perfection gradually as God draws humanity back to Himself. In other words, if God were to instantly restore the created order, it would collapse upon itself due to its complexity. So the only way to safely allow for the restoration without wiping out all the creatures within creation is to segment it into dimensions. This is my theory anyway," Genesis muses with a smirk, then continues, "Each dimension adds to the previous ones. With each added dimension, the person who holds consciousness in a way gains a separation from the previous dimensions. So, in a physical manner with the first three dimensions, then in a spiritual manner thereafter.

"Concerning the first three dimensions—these are the ones which are intuitively known and accessible to common humans. Humans can intuitively sense the first three dimensions: length, width and height. So to understand these three, we must look to the animal world. After all, animals vary in their perception to a level which is mostly inferior to humans. Humans were ever intended to be physical creatures, like animals, yet possessing spiritual capabilities to move them beyond the merely physical world. So, to explain the first three dimensions, we need to use examples from the rudimentary animal kingdom.

"Beginning with the 1st dimension: *length*. A 1st dimension creature is brutish and direct. An animal who operates within 1st dimension thinking is a creature who thinks linearly. In other words, a 1st dimension animal sees what it needs, then moves toward it in a forward line. Upon receiving what it desires, the brutish animal then thinks of what it needs next, then moves toward it. This is similar to an ox, or other beasts of burden, such as cattle. It is not to say they do not use the 2nd or 3rd dimensions of physical width or height. Rather it is to say that cattle has no need to ponder on such things. Cattle simply perceives what it needs, in this case the desire for food, water, mating, et cetera, and in each case, the animal moves toward it. The animal continues in this process, moment after moment, for its entire life—stopping linear pursuit only when another interest becomes more pressing. In this case, the beast who is chewing grass will continue to do so until thirst for water surpasses his sense of hunger. Then the animal will move toward water. Very little can interrupt this cycle of operation for a 1st dimension creature. If they sense a predator, for example, they will override this 1st dimension process for a moment until they escape. Or if their herd begins to move, then they will move with it. In this way, the 1st dimension beast for brief moments holds a 2nd dimension awareness—being concerning for survival sake of the events occurring to their right or left. However, their concern with the 2nd dimension quickly fleets, as they resume normal 1st dimension operations. Even in the case that one of their herd members is killed by a predator, the other 1st dimension cattle will remain unaffected. As their counterpart is being eaten mere meters away, the other cattle quietly slips back into its 1st dimension patterns— being entirely unconcerned and unaware of the pain experienced by their counterpart. The general self-talk for 1st dimension creatures would be akin to: '*I'm hungry—I eat food. I'm thirsty—I drink water.*' There is nothing inherently bad about 1st dimension creatures. They are existing as they have been designed to exist.

"Concerning the 2nd dimension—*width*. A 2nd dimension creature is social—being concerned with its pack or the members of its group. In this level of perception, the creature thinks about the other members of its pack to its right and left—hence 'width.' Examples include lions and wolves. A 2nd dimension creature maintains concern for other members—being capable of communication amongst its fellow members. Often, these 2nd dimension creatures will even mourn the deaths of its fellows. Very prominent examples of this include elephants and dolphins. Whereas a herd of cattle remains entirely unconcerned with the death of one of its own, 2nd dimension animals care for one another. At times they can be cruel with one another, but ultimately, the beasts with 2nd dimension capability remain ever conscious of the other members of their group—present to their right and left. Within 2nd dimension thinking, individuals may have brief glimpses of 3rd dimension thought. For example, individuals may seek to gain prominence as an alpha within the pack—thus gaining figurative height above the common members. But in this sense, these creatures typically do not maintain a long-standing 3rd dimension view where they constantly assess the pack itself. Rather, a strong lion may fight and win for itself '*alpha*' status, but upon winning this achievement it quickly resumes its normal 2nd dimension patterns. The general self-talk for 2nd dimension creatures would be akin to: '*I'm hungry, we're hungry, we hunt, we eat, I eat.*' Thus, within the 2nd dimension creature's concern for the pack they also find fulfillment for themselves.

"Concerning the 3rd dimension—*height*. An example of a 3rd dimension animal is the eagle. This is not saying the eagle is mentally more advanced than 2nd

dimension social animals. Intelligence as we define it doesn't necessarily correlate with dimensional capability. However, eagles are more advanced dimensionally in the sense that they soar above the world below them— assessing and choosing where they will interact with the world they see. Thus, the eagle is not subject to danger thrust upon them in the normal manner which can afflict 1st and 2nd dimension beasts. The eagle is separate and above. Concerning certain birds, they can perceive the actions of animals below them, predicting secondary effects. So, birds will follow herds. Birds are opportunistic, seeing things from the safety of height, then swooping in at just the right moments. They gain and maintain situational awareness. In this way, the 3rd dimension animal transcends the normal limits imposed on 1st and 2nd dimension beasts. Their extra dimension grants them nearly a nearly limitless area of safety— buffering themselves from the dangerous world below them. . . . As we consider this, the rudimentary form of humans would be identified as 3rd dimension. Humans create buffer zones to separate themselves from the dangerous natural world around them. Although humans cannot naturally fly, they use other means to create buffer zones—including: houses, fences, weapons, fire. They further insulate themselves against harm by using agriculture and shepherding in an attempt to ward off the basic threat of hunger. The procedure for 3rd dimension creatures, including 3rd dimension humans, would involve a toggling between safety, surveillance, assessment and opportunistic achievement. On a basic level, 3rd dimension thinking involves maintaining safety, then stepping out of that safety at opportunistic moments before resuming safety. Humans that are 3rd dimensional can show brief glimpses of 4th dimension thinking in their spirituality, arts and academic pursuits, however a human who is 3rd dimensional will roughly adhere to the same procedures of the eagle.

"Concerning the 4th dimension—'*in/out*.' Although the phrase, 'in/out,' is inadequate to describe this physically hidden dimension, this phrase does well in communicating the basic concept. With the 4th dimension, a human gains the ability to see objects in their fuller existence. Objects viewed in the 3rd dimension may actually be a part of a much larger 4th dimension object. This is especially true in the case of Luminary Systems and their Luminaries, in addition to the appearances of their magnetic north center points. So, with the gaining of 4th dimension capabilities, one becomes endowed with the ability to see things as they really are, rather than just the partial picture contained within the 3rd dimension. Thus, to the human with 4th dimension capability, the 3rd dimension appears like a prison—encasing others in a partial, merely physical reality. As a human nears 4th dimension capability, this sense of imprisonment or being trapped can grow within the 3rd dimension human. They begin to see the world around them as barring them in ethereally. Once a person perceives this, the human mind seeks a means to shake itself free. It is around this time a human can become capable of experiencing the *in/out*, 4th dimension capability—gaining access to the Luminary Watchhand. Their mind then separates from the chains which previously fixed it in place. It is my conviction that humans were always intended to operate on at least the 4th dimension level. I think humans were corrupted at what the Bible calls the "fall." At that time, humans experienced a regression in their thinking—causing humans to slip into the 3rd dimension as their rudimentary state. However, from the beginning, the Creator never intended humans to be limited to the 3rd dimension. This is apparent in the fact that the Bible says humans were all made in the image of God. Therefore, God always desired for humans to be near Him. God always desired humans to be within creation, similar in physical form to animals, yet capable of seeing inside and outside of it. So, the 4th dimension should be understood as the intended, rudimentary dimension of humans.

"Concerning the 5th dimension—'*tilt forward/tilt backward*.' These are my personal thoughts based on my single experience—having verified no other humans as 5th dimension capable. . . . In my experience of time travel, where I moved three-thousand years into the future, I sensed I tilted forward on the Luminary Watchhand—allowing me to see Luminary Systems below me fragment into endless, repeating sequences of near mirror images. After having arrived in this Luminary System in current year, I now realize what I saw when I experienced the tilt. Perhaps each replication of the Luminary Systems below me were various snapshots in time, capturing how that specific Luminary System appeared at precise times. Without realizing or controlling this process, I was somehow placed within this current Luminary System. As we delve further into thoughts of the 5th dimension, we can anticipate many advancements as we learn more. It is my conviction the 5th dimension is an angelic dimension. Angels, by definition, are messengers from God. I view the 5th dimension as the corridors through which God's angels pass throughout Creation. In the Bible, 'Jacob's ladder' could be a reference to the use of the 5th dimension. Just as I am convinced the 4th dimension was designed as the intended rudimentary realm of human operation, I am convinced the 5th dimension was designed as the rudimentary realm of angel operation. It is not to say that certain beings are confined to a specific dimension. We know we can move further, and are intended to move further—as evidenced by Bible prophets who participated in a type of time travel, clearly viewing and relaying future events. However, the 5th dimension should be viewed as the realm of various kinds of divine messengers. The Bible provides us an ancient witness that this 5th dimension is indeed open to humans. This being the case, I think humans will only be capable of using the 5th dimension through an Angelic Conduit. An Angelic Conduit is either an angel or a human with the ability to courier others in the 5th dimension. It appears I may be an Angelic Conduit—as evidenced by my verified ability to throw documents back in time from the Luminary Watchhand. Currently, I have a plan in place to validate my theory further. I plan to send a human volunteer back in time to myself in the 21st Century. I think my 21st Century self may be capable of bringing back the volunteer with him. Once my theory is validated, it will advance our understanding of the 5th dimension and guide our planning efforts for future missions to the past.

"Last, at the end of my thoughts and theories—for now anyway—is the 6th dimension. At time of publication, the 6th dimension is completely uncharted and theoretical. Yet, if I am correct—and I tend to be correct about such matters," Genesis states with a smirk, "I believe the 6th dimension may be one which is totally independent of physical forms—where the things of the lower dimensions are somehow represented by images, yet where humans can move in completely spiritual form. This is all connected to my theories on Wanderers and my research as an Accessions Commander. In my study of ancient Israelite texts, I found a class of visionaries called 'prophets.' Among the prophets some had the ability to be spiritually transported to a higher realm of Heaven. While present in Heaven, their physical bodies would remain on Earth. Once in Heaven, the prophet would see events which would appear in apocalyptic form—where spiritual items represented events and items found in the physical dimensions. This was very common in the Bible—with even the items from their temple of worship being made after Heavenly patterns. In other words, these prophets were not simply travelling to the future—which would have been 5th dimensional and similar to the movement of angels. In the Bible, angels often would move throughout the Earth in a form which was at least partially physical. This means physical time travel is 5th dimensional. But the prophets would move to places where they could leave their bodies behind altogether—where events occurred as images. I think this is the 6th dimension.

"Furthermore, I can support my view with my Inversely Proportional Dimensional Consciousness theory, which states: '*All human souls have similar potential as the image of God, so the vitality of an incapacitated or partially incapacitated human must be present elsewhere.*'

"When encountering a person who appears mentally incapacitated in the 3rd dimension, we can be confident the vitality of their soul is present with their full consciousness elsewhere. To suppose otherwise would be to wrongly assume that either the person has no spirit and is a lesser human than others, or that God somehow gave them a defective soul—both options are wrong, of course. Rather, I am confident these incapacitated humans are merely operating on a different dimension of existence— similar to the out-of-body movement of prophets in the Heavenly realms. So, in my thoughts about the 6th dimension, I am hopeful we will one day discover many Wanderers. The more incapacitated the individual appears in the 3rd dimension may indicate their vast advancement in the totally spiritual realm of the 6th dimension. When the vitality of the person is not fully present with the person's body, it must be existing elsewhere in powerful form. In my theory, I am hopeful we will one day encounter these same individuals within the 6th dimension. Although they are in a lesser form in the 3rd dimension, upon our arrival in the 6th dimension we may find these humans have already accomplished great achievements. I think these individuals are firmly established in the 6th dimension and likely working in discovery of the 7th, 8th and maybe even the 9th dimension. So, once we reach the 6th dimension—if I am correct, we may be able to join with them and immediately jump several dimensions in advancement. It is an exciting prospect!"

After listening intently, Kai finally emerges from his notes. His interest is captured by Genesis' discussion of the 6th dimension.

"Genesis, I have never heard of this before."

"Kai, it is what happens when you spend all your time reading ancient books," Genesis muses. His reply evoked an outward gasp from Kai—signaling his astonishment at Genesis' seeming dismissal of his own wisdom. His teaching was so profound it threatened pulling all humanity in its wake. And, even more profound—as humanity would soon realize—the pilgrim's teaching was surpassed by his determination and abilities.

Kai takes a deep breath. He realizes he has forgotten to breathe for quite some time—being ever pulled further into the words of the pilgrim as he spoke. Kai's breath stirs his vision. The air rattles free a reflection from his mind . . .

"Genesis, I was thinking, if the mentally incapacitated people in the 3rd dimension are really advanced in the 6th dimension and beyond, then they are just working in reverse from us."

"What do you mean, Kai?"

"Well, whereas our progress has been halted at the 5th dimension, these humans' progress was halted at the 3rd dimension. So, just as we might need them to teach us about the 6th, 7th and 8th if they arrived, these advanced humans will need us to teach them about the 3rd and 4th dimensions. Remarkably, those easy dimensions for us might be their biggest challenge." Kai waits for a moment. He is so jumbled by his own use of numbers that he fears he lost Genesis somehow in his transactions.

Genesis however was right on his trail, "Exactly, Kai. At the pinnacle of the 6th dimension, humanity will advance by learning to put the last, first—honoring those who were least recognized in the 3rd dimension. Although it is no longer common to see, at the time when I first lived there were so many people with disabilities. It was absolutely heartbreaking to see these poor childr--."

Genesis trails off as tears obscure his vision: First at the bottom, then filling to the top. His heart sank, forming a well which seemed as if it were drawing tears downward to fill itself. The pilgrim's mind is filled with images from his previous life—absolutely wrenching his heart. As his mind was ushered into its past, Genesis' heart writhed—as if it were a washcloth catching tears, wringing itself out with every heartbeat, only to draw in more tears. The pilgrim was moved deeply by the grief experienced by humans in the ancient world—so much pain, all without answers, abandoned to itself. The old world collapsing upon itself in futility—having no restoration or recourse for the most basic harms which afflicted it.

Now, just as quickly as the pilgrim's heart descended into grief for the past, a fire from within overwhelms him. A surge of power passes through his body—drawing supernatural strength to the surface, causing him to tense his arms as he held back the surge in other parts. His back radiates a rush of heat—passing across his shoulders, racing throughout his body. The cascading electricity within tightens Genesis' perception—most notably pulling his sight of the room inward upon itself. His mind blasts through visions of humanity's future restoration—as all those who were lost are reunited with their perfected physical bodies. He sees a vast healing in store for humanity in his generation as a shadow of the resurrection at the Last Day.

The moment passes as Genesis emerges, thankful for the vision—giving him courage for the journey ahead. The pilgrim recaptures his mind and completes his thought . . .

"Kai, people who appear incapacitated in the 3rd dimension are really just operating on a different level—

being far advanced within another dimension, likely completing projects which we cannot fathom and upon which humanity will utterly depend once we break into the 6th dimension."

Genesis pauses as his heart is still stirring, imploring him return to the vision he saw within his mind. He has an abiding sense that he missed something important. The pilgrim's mind is drawing his attention—beckoning him to move inward to see something further. As Genesis moves within the fortress of his mind, preparing to close the door behind him, he concludes with endearment—hoping above all this will stick as a memory within Kai's mind:

"My dear Kai, we need everyone. Every human is valuable to us. This is our journey. We need to understand this. We need to break free from the past judgments that ruined humanity. We need to learn to see within the souls of broken people—rather than assuming they are just broken shells. Unless we do this, we are doomed. I know that is why I was brought here. We must all learn from the disasters I witnessed. That is the path before us, my dear Kai . . . We will find them."

8

Ancient Human Integration in 5000 A.D.

Kai Anthropos-Anthropos looks up to see the pilgrim seated before him. Kai is then reminded of his purpose. This session is scheduled to discuss how humans from the past may be assimilated into his own 5000 A.D. culture. Kai is drawn to this meeting—feeling a profound sense of responsibility. He thinks of the great task which will be placed upon the people of his society as they are called to extend hospitality to travelers from all corners of humanity's distant past.

At first, Kai begins to feel overwhelmed. As his mind swirls over different thoughts, with many causing collisions with other thoughts, Kai is comforted by the presence of Genesis. Across the table, the pilgrim appears stern and laser-focused. Surely, if anyone could solve the challenges posed by the arrival of ancient time travelers, it must be the visionary before him. Thus, Kai begins the discussion.

"It is nice to see you again, Genesis."

"It is nice to see you as well, Kai Anthropos-Anthropos."

"Sorry, I did not hear you walk in."

"No worries, my friend. I have a habit of showing up unannounced." Genesis' comment was a veiled reference to his time travel arrival in 5000 A.D. In that case, the pilgrim snuck up on an entire society unawares.

It was an entertaining mental picture for the pilgrim to consider. He often told jokes to himself within his mind. At times he would laugh aloud at himself—evoking queries from bystanders as to the event which beckoned his laughter forth. Genesis would always dismiss the questions as he retreated back within his own mind. It was one thing to be comfortable when alone; the pilgrim, however, was so comfortable alone he would entertain himself with his own jokes.

In this case, Kai caught the veiled joke. But Kai was intent on learning today. He set aside the joke—eager to coach Genesis in productive conversation . . .

"Genesis, today we are scheduled to discuss human integration in 5000 A.D. If you would like, please feel free to begin. I will listen and take notes." At this point, Kai was unsure where the future would find him. He reasoned this conversation would give him the information he would need to best prepare himself. *Who knows?* Kai mused to himself, *I might be one of the humans who hosts a new arrival.* The thought caused a warmth to spread over Kai. The prospect of receiving an ancient human like David to whom he could show practical kindness and support was comforting. Kai reflected on Genesis' words in his book on David—that it is possible David lived his entire life without the receipt of practical human concern, being lost within his own mind with no one who understood him. Kai was not sure why, but this thought alone made him feel like crying— imagining the common suffering endured by ancient humans, which they bore faithfully with no hope of recourse in their time. Kai was lifted by the prospect that he may in fact become an answer to ancient prayers uttered in the midst of hardship and long forgotten by all others. Kai was enthusiastic. Although he was taking notes for the interview, most of all he was taking notes to prepare himself.

"Thank you, Kai," Genesis answered as he began, "Our goal within the Accessions Command is to identify ancient humans with skills which are valuable to our 5000 A.D. society. This involves research into all areas of past humans—reading books, processing data and so on.

Anything which provides insight on humanity's history will be examined. Once we identify specific individuals for potential transport, we will prepare and send out Task Forces into these past half-bubbles in the 5th dimension."

Genesis' military background makes him eager to discuss how these Task Forces will be organized, trained and how they will execute missions. Genesis falls silent in the room as he interacts with these thoughts within his own mind. A moment later, the awkward silence is broken by Kai as he attempts to call forth Genesis from silence.

"Genesis, when these ancient humans arrive in our society, how will we integrate them?"

The words allow the pilgrim to break contact within himself. Genesis is thankful for the question. It is indeed a broad topic and quite easy to become distracted by red herrings.

"Kai, although this is an uncharted venture for which we have no data, we can predict one of our greatest challenges will be Perception Overload."

"What's that?"

"In my estimation, Perception Overload may occur if ancient humans are not granted a gradual assimilation process. We must remember these humans are from completely different times. So, to place them amongst our citizens immediately may cause them to have many problems. To prevent Perception Overload, we plan to have areas where we can help these ancient humans to be completely comfortable in their surroundings as they are slowly introduced to our society."

"That makes sense."

"Yes, it does. I remember how overwhelmed I felt when realizing I was in this new place."

Kai remembers not too long ago when Genesis first arrived in their half-bubble. He is somewhat embarrassed within himself to have not first considered Genesis' experience adjusting to society after his time jump.

"What was the adjustment like for you, Genesis?"

"It was challenging, Kai," Genesis is thankful for Kai's concern, but he desires to keep the discussion broad, "As you know, humans are very complicated. Our minds are great tools, but at times they can even hinder us in our circumstances. The last thing we would want to do is damage the fragile mental ability within the ancient human by exposing them to things for which they are not prepared." Genesis continues, "The best way I can explain Perception Overload, would be by explaining shock. When a person experiences an injury, they may be capable of surviving the injury itself, but if the mind is not treated for shock, the person might not survive."

"What do you mean?"

"Think about it: If I have a very bad cut on my body, I might be okay if I remain calm. But if I begin to think negative thoughts about how I may die, then this will cause my heart to race. In this case, my mental shock may cause my heart to race further—in turn causing my bleeding to worsen," Genesis pauses, then attempts another example, "Or if I am bitten by a viper, I may be okay if I remain calm during transportation to a hospital. But if I allow my mind to stress in the situation—thinking about how I might die, then my heart would begin racing. So, the mental shock may cause my body to circulate the venom even faster—reducing my chance of survival."

"I understand," Kai answers.

"Perception Overload is very similar to shock. Although an ancient person may survive their journey to us, we must help them manage their thoughts during their adjustment. In fact, for many people the adjustment might not even be possible—and the attempt would be most cruel in those cases."

Kai's silence and accompanying gestures signal his lack of understanding. Genesis perceives Kai's quandary as he guides him further . . .

"For example, if a person is accustomed to a lifelong wife or husband, the separation from their mate might be sufficient to cause Perception Overload from which the individual may not recover. Indeed, the individual may begin to resent us for proposing their transport in the first place. In this case, a most useful, skilled individual who is not evaluated for the possibility of Perception Overload may result in a very bad fit for our society. So, we need to identify skilled individuals who are most likely to overcome the challenges of Perception Overload."

"Interesting," Kai answers, "How did you do it, Genesis? . . . How did you avoid Perception Overload?" Kai is persistent in his pursuit to hear the pilgrim's story.

"Well, the mind of a person should be a major concern in our choice of whether or not to propose transport to an individual. Frankly, I was able to adjust rapidly due to my military background and 'post-traumatic stress disorder,' also known as PTSD. In my past life, I spent many years just barely surviving. This made it where I became accustomed to somehow finding a way in whatever situation I found myself. The military also transferred humans to different surroundings often, so I never grew accustomed to people as permanent fixtures in my life," Genesis continues, "Even in the case of family, I never grew accustomed to always having specific people near me because I was always having to leave on missions. Beyond this, my PTSD—similar to David, made me capable of constantly seeing beyond my physical circumstances. All these factors combined to give me the ability to overcome Perception Overload. Honestly, you could probably place me just about anywhere, and over time my mind would adapt to it."

"You are a strong person, Genesis."

"I wouldn't go too far, Kai," Genesis retreats from the compliment, "We all have strengths and different quirks. No one is completely strong or perfect, apart from Christ. Whereas I may be strong in one area, those strengths result in weaknesses in other areas," Genesis holds up his walking cane so the top peaks over the table top—a non-verbal illustration of his point. "We may be strong in certain areas, but we also have challenges which accompany those strengths. . . . This lends to my understanding of humanity as a whole—we all need each other. If all of us offered our strengths to the benefit of others, then we would finally become capable of overcoming *all* the weaknesses."

Kai nods, "So if strong people have challenges, then it is okay for everyone else to admit to them as well."

"Yes, we shouldn't hide from those things which make us different. Often within weaknesses strength is hidden. We just need the wisdom to see how each weakness provides strength."

"That is just like your theory of the 6th dimension, right?"

"Right. Those humans whose bodies are broken in the 3rd dimension are due to their vast advancement in greater dimensions. All humans have similar soul vitality—and if it is not present in one dimension, it must be present in another. I am convinced of this. This is the principle on which the concept of Afterlife depends." Genesis was thankful for this red herring. He was always pleased to briefly offer this thought—at every possible occasion. After an entire lifetime of viewing the mistreatment of 'differently-abled' people in the 21st Century, Genesis always desired an opportunity to challenge this ghost of the past. Indeed, he thought, his words may become a constant check upon the future of humanity—preventing future humans from adopting this failed modus operandi from the 21st Century.

Kai reels in the conversation, "Genesis, once Perception Overload is accounted for, what are some other things to consider concerning the importing of ancient humans?"

"Kai, the process of integration will all depend on the individual. For example, when an ancient human arrives, they may be placed among a community of people in a forest area similar to their past surroundings. Over time, it may be gradually revealed to them certain details of the 5000 A.D. society beyond it."

"What if the person does not respond well to gradual integration?"

"In some cases, the individuals may in effect choose to remain within the forest community—in our example. Of course, this would be okay. An ancient person may not desire to move into a large city—that is fine."

"What about teaching the person about our society?" Kai asks.

"In the overall scheme, teaching the individual about our society may be unnecessary. Of course, the human could choose to study our history, customs, language and arts, but there would be no requirement to do so. Remember, the mission of the Accessions Command is to bring skilled individuals to us so that we can learn from them. If the ancient human desires to teach from the seclusion of their quiet, forest retreat away from our cities, then that is fine. Indeed, it might be better if they did so."

"What do you mean?"

"People become who they are because of their past situations. So, to imagine an ancient visionary may be capable of remaining a visionary in different types of surroundings would be unreasonable. For all we know, exposing an ancient visionary to the wonders of our society may cause them to fall away from their past visionary behavior. It would be a tragedy indeed to bring an ancient visionary to a place where their outstanding ability is somehow corrupted by circumstances and subsequently used for negative purpose. We must always remember many of these ancient visionaries may have lived in seclusion, so allowing them to maintain a setting similar to their past may be a critical component to their purpose within the Accessions Command."

"I see."

"Throughout the process, the Accessions Command will need to make sure the ancient visionaries are comfortable in their new settings. We will need representatives with them who are responsive to their adjustment processes."

"Genesis, how will the ancient humans teach us?"

"Well, today we still have many of the documents and evidence that tells us about these people. Indeed, these historical records are how we will find each of them. So, we will not need these ancient humans to teach us things we already know—or can learn from reading about it for ourselves in historical records. Instead, we need these ancient visionaries to teach us specifically how to do what they learned to do."

"Practical teaching?" Kai summarizes Genesis.

"Yes, practical teaching—similar to apprenticeships . . . learning from these visionaries the lost skills which humanity may need to encounter our next Frontiers. Wherever the specific visionary chooses to live, people can go to them and learn."

"How will ancient humans be selected for transport?"

"The Accessions Commanders review historical records to identify individuals—giving priority to those who will be low risk for Perception Overload. Then the Accessions Command will send documents back to the individual via an embedded Task Force. Only if an individual is willing to be imported will they be transferred to 5000 A.D. We will not take anyone unless they are willing to be transported. Ultimately it would defeat our purpose to transport a human to teach us a lost skill when they are unwilling to teach our future society."

"Genesis, you said ancient humans who are low risk for Perception Overload. How would they be assessed?"

"Within the historical records, Accessions Commanders will make a likely assessment based on details about the individual. For example, if an individual spent many years on a battlefield, in the case of David, then we could be reasonably assured they would not buckle while learning to adjust to our society. But in cases where it is not easily discernable, the embedded Task Force who delivers our documents to the individual will make the assessment. Of course, an ancient human would not have a high probability of overcoming Perception Overload if they are transported during a crisis in their previous life, or if they are in the process of waiting for a certain event. So, the Task Force leader would assist in making that determination with the identified individual," Genesis pauses. The pilgrim had a habit of over-explaining. Rather than going overboard with unnecessary details, carrying Kai in his wake, Genesis checks for acceptance, "I hope that is helpful."

"It is, Genesis," Kai says as he flips a page. After pausing to view another page, Kai appears satisfied with the discussion. "It looks like we covered all the topics for this session. I hope you have a nice day, Genesis."

The pilgrim smiled.

9

Time Travel Missions to the Past

"Hello, Genesis, it is good to see you again."

"Greetings, Kai Aetos-Anthropos, it has been a while since we last spoke."

"Yes, I am happy to have another opportunity to speak with you. During today's session we are scheduled to discuss time travel missions to the past." Kai adds, "I am particularly interested in this topic. My goal is to one day oversee a mission to the past."

"That is a noble goal, Kai. I believe you can do it," Genesis smiles.

"Thank you," Kai returns the expression.

"Well, as I explained in earlier discussions, the 3rd dimension aspect is 'height.' I think of this dimension as one of perspective—where the eagle is able to soar above and view events carefully as they unfold below. I think you are especially well-suited for *overseeing* operations, Kai Aetos-Anthropos," Genesis says as he gestures to the avian physical enhancements of Kai.

"Thank you, Genesis," Kai swells with healthy pride—gaining inner resolve and confidence from the well-placed words of the pilgrim. He quickly shifts in his seat, directing his sharpened vision across the table—as if he is peering *through* Genesis, eagerly desiring to examine every word the moment it forms on his lips. As he causes a ruffle to pass throughout his body, Kai speaks further, "Genesis, please feel free to continue by discussing team missions to the past. I will try not to interrupt."

"Okay, this is a topic which I enjoy very much, so please forgive me if I speak too much. By the time we are finished, you and our readers should have a good understanding of the Accessions Command's basic operational structure." Genesis pauses, then begins his journey of explanation . . .

"First, each Accessions Command has a Commander. It is the Commander's responsibility to research a specific time and region in human history. The goal is to identify ancient humans who may have possessed skills which are no longer present in our 5000

A.D. society. Currently, I can only send documents—books, letters—back in time. Soon, however, I hope to test my ability to send humans back and forth in time. Once acquiring and testing this ability, my goal is to send teams to retrieve certain humans.

"Second, within the Accessions Command, the Commander has Task Forces employed to execute retrievals. Each Task Force consists of a Task Force Leader and three teams. Each team is identical in composition: having a Dimension Specialist for each dimension—1st, 2nd, 3rd, 4th, and 5th—once we figure out the 5th dimension that is," Genesis smirks—a wry smile, as a nod to the inherent mystery still present within the concept of time travel. "I suppose once we figure out the 6th dimension, each team will need a 6th Dimension Specialist as well—but we just aren't there yet.

Genesis continues, "The three teams of each Task Force are redundant in structure. The idea is that the teams can support one another within their retrieval mission. If, for example, you and I were both Team Leaders, and something happened to your 4th Dimension Specialist, then your team could simply combine with mine."

"That is a good idea," Kai concedes.

"Yes," Genesis answers, "This allows each Task Force to be prepared for reasonable contingencies. The last thing we would want is for a team to become stranded. This concept goes all the way back to the days of Earth ocean navigation. Whereas damage to a single

165

boat would be devastating to the crew; the use of multiple boats travelling together allowed for the ability to consolidate. If one boat started to sink, the crew still had another boat to board. Therefore, in our approach to time travel and retrieval, we plan to have three teams move with one another to provide mutual support."

Kai jostles between his seat and the table, "Genesis, please explain the 'Dimension Specialists.' What is a 1st Dimension Specialist?" Kai finished his point, peering further into the issue, "How can a 3rd dimension human be a 1st Dimension Specialist?"

"Yeah, that is a funny thought right? . . . As if a human could just be 1st dimensional," Genesis laughs—a gesture matched in kind by Kai. "No, it is not to say that the Dimension Specialist would be limited to that respective dimension. Rather it is to point out the focus of each person within the team. Remember, the 1st dimension corresponds to 'length.' Much like a beast with 1st dimension thinking, this specialist would be focused on obtaining provisions, like food and other supplies, for the team. The 1st Dimension Specialist devotes their efforts toward obtaining daily provisions and shelter for the entire team. Essentially, this specialist is the logistic expert who provides for the physical needs of the team. . . . Then, the 2nd Dimension Specialist would be concerned with 'width'—similar to a social animal with 2nd dimension thinking, who perceives its fellows to its left and right. Thus, the 2nd Dimension Specialist would be concerned with attending to the personal concerns of team members, in addition to coordinating with humans outside the team."

"In other words, the 2nd Dimension Specialist would likely be the leader of each team?" Kai summarizes.

"Yes. Or at least the team members and humans outside the team would perceive the 2nd Dimension Specialist this way. This is the person who is primarily concerned with communication. Similar to social pack animals, the 2nd Dimension Specialist would also serve as the security expert within the team—ensuring measures are taken and maintained to protect all the individuals. In other words, think of the 2nd Dimension Specialist as the alpha lion in the pride roaming amidst the other lions, checking them, and who is roused at necessary times to defend the entire pride."

"Genesis, the 4th Dimension Specialist would be self-explanatory—a person with advanced 4th dimension ability, but what would a 3rd Dimension Specialist do?"

"Kai, the 3rd Dimension Specialist is involved in team operation oversight. Similar to a bird with 3rd dimension thinking—this specialist looks at the operation of the team from the 3rd dimension of 'height,' to ensure everyone is doing their mission in the best possible way. Usually this will be a person trained to identify problems and increase efficiency. This specialist would communicate directly with the Task Force Leader. So essentially, each 3rd Dimension Specialist is a direct representative for the Task Force Leader, ensuring team activity will integrate with the other teams."

"Wow. That is a lot more complex than I thought it would be."

"It seems that way, but as I explained the structure directly corresponds to each dimension. Essentially, the dimensions themselves tell us exactly how to structure each team," Genesis chuckles, "Indeed we can learn much from observing the animal world around us."

It is a simple observation, but it captures Kai. At this moment, Kai considers how much wisdom escapes us simply because we do not have the wisdom to perceive it. For now, Kai recoils from this thought.

"What about a 5th Dimension Specialist?"

"A 5th Dimension Specialist would be a person capable of 5th dimension 'time travel.' In my theory, this may or may not be a human."

"What do you mean?"

"Well, from my research in the Bible, it appears many prophets achieved some form of time travel— allowing them to predict future events. In some cases, these predictive visions of the future were ushered to the prophet by angels. So, my theory is we may meet certain types of angels as we move into the 5th dimension."

"Huh?"

"It is just my theory for now, but I think this is the direction being revealed in the dimensions. Whereas dimensions 1, 2 and 3 correspond to physical reality; the 4th dimension corresponds to the spiritual reality which contains the physical. Then the 5th dimension captures the development of time throughout the lower dimensions. After this the 6th dimension is one in which the vitality of human souls can operate independent of their physical bodies—where 6th dimension events are created to be superimposed upon dimensions 1-5. Then the 7th dimens---"

"Oh, I see," Kai interrupts. His mouth appears as if it is beginning to form a question, but being unsure what to ask, he settles for a nod—signaling the pilgrim to continue.

Genesis shifts, retreating back to his discussion of angels, "In the Bible we are told there are different types of angels—having different appearances and roles within Heaven. The meaning of the word 'angel' is 'messenger.' So, it is my thought that just as angel messengers served as couriers for ancient prophets, perhaps angels may receive divine instructions to help us in our missions to the past and back to the present."

"Very cool."

"It is. Every time humans advance forward in these dimensions it is likely we will always experience revelations just as exciting. The jumps between dimensions are vast. Although it seems extraordinary now for us to interact with angels, I think this is exactly what we should expect in the 5th dimension. Along with this hope we do exercise wisdom. We know there are fallen angels, also known as demons, and we must be wary of this," Genesis digresses.

"What other challenges are posed along with the possibility of working with angels?"

"Well, the Task Forces themselves will need to train to encounter cultural differences, language barriers and so on in their target mission areas. Similarly, the Task Force Leader may be required to be an individual capable of communication with the assigned 5th dimension angel—if we must travel with angels. At this point we do not know for sure though. It might be that humans themselves will become capable of advancing their own 5th dimension abilities, becoming Angelic Conduits—making assignment of an angel unnecessary. Frankly we do not know for sure yet."

"This is making my head hurt," Kai states as he motions his hand over his skull—as if to persuade his brain to remain within.

"Welcome to my world," Genesis retorts with a smirk. "This is all I do: I read ancient documents and I ponder how far we can reach in all directions. However, when we have the skill to consider such things, it is our responsibility to do so. Many human advancements have been altogether lost in history—resulting in dead ends as real as those on the Luminary Watchhand. Today, we should be wary of abandoning our pursuit of further revelation. Indeed, future generations may depend on our inquiries." Genesis summarizes, "We can figure it out—we must simply stay the course. We move as far as we can in one direction, then continue to move forward in another. To be a visionary, one must risk being wrong."

Kai smiles.

"To pick up where I left off, Kai, concerning each Dimension Specialist, they will be provided with specific training to help them in their duties. Then in the time leading up to Task Force's deployment, they will conduct practice exercises and pass assessments. Overall, we will not send out a Task Force unless it is well-prepared for its mission. New Task Forces will be evaluated in their training by previously successful Task Force Leaders."

"That is good to know," Kai agrees.

"Yes. By the way, did I explain yet about why there are three teams in each Task Force?"

"No, not yet, Genesis."

"Okay. This is important: When a Task Force is deployed on a mission, the three teams are capable of rotating within their tasks. This makes it possible for a Task Force to endure long term."

"I have heard of this before. You discuss this in your David book, right?"

"Right. Even from ancient times, military commanders would often organize units based on the number three. This makes it possible to rotate troops in and out of the most difficult areas of the battlefield. Sticking with this principle, each Task Force Leader will employ the three assigned teams based on this principle."

"How does the rotation work?"

Genesis answers, "Well, in its deployment, the Task Force will be required to maintain the following three areas: *Anchor Team, Insertion Team, and Surveillance Team.*

"Concerning the Anchor Team, the Task Force Leader will ensure one team remains on the Luminary Watchhand. When a team is assigned as the Task Force anchor, they do not move—no matter what. This ensures that the teams which move off the Luminary Watchhand will not be stuck within a Luminary System due to an unforeseen contingency. The Anchor Team also retrieves document drops from positions on the Luminary Watchhand—but they do not move off the Luminary Watchhand.

"Concerning the Insertion Team, this is the team which moves within a past Luminary System to retrieve a human. This is the operational team of the Task Force.

"Last, the Surveillance Team is responsible for moving as a courier between the Anchor Team and the Insertion Team. In its duties, the Surveillance Team also monitors situations and conditions which may affect the Insertion Team, in addition to providing support.

"This trifold structure is not only based on previous military operations, but it also corresponds to my research of the Bible and the nature of God. As in my research, I found God the Father as the *anchor* Person of the Trinity—who ever remains transcendent beyond the entire created order, holding within Himself all knowledge. God the Son is the *insertion* Person of the Trinity who moves within the created order to provide salvation for humanity through His death and resurrection

172

in the New Testament. Throughout the Old Testament, however, the Son moves in and out of the created order, appearing at many times in human form to various people. If the Lord in a passage has a physical, human body, then this must be the Son. Also, the Son depends on the Father for knowledge and guidance in His earthly activity. So, to easily determine the identity of the Son in the Old Testament, one must merely find clues connected to God's presumed 'lack of knowledge.' If it appears the Lord in a passage does not know something, then this passage is simply referring to the Son—examples include the Lord Jesus not knowing about the fig tree, the day of His return, who will sit on His right and left and so on. There are many examples of a similar lack of knowledge in the Old Testament—and it should be understood that all such passages are referring to the Son, who depends upon the Father for knowledge. Last, the Holy Spirit is the *surveillance* Person of the Trinity who moves as courier between the other two Persons, while also providing direct support to the Son. The Holy Spirit maintains creation itself from this surveillance position. So, you will find the structure of each Task Force is designed to mirror the inner efficiency of the Lord God. All three are united in purpose, yet different in their tasks as they mutually support one another." Although Genesis desires to continue in his discussion of the Trinity model upon which his Task Forces are structured, he digresses, "It is a very broad topic, but I assure you it is based on a well-established, mutually-supporting, successful pattern."

"That is very interesting, Genesis." Kai shifts the discussion, "So what would the Task Force do if it ran into a problem?"

"What kind of problem, Kai?"

"God forbid, but let's say something happened to a Dimension Specialist or something like that."

"Well, in that case, the Task Force Leader would receive a report from the Surveillance Team. Then the Task Force Leader would shift personnel. The top priority is always to maintain a complete Anchor Team on the Luminary Watchhand. This means that non-essential personnel from the Surveillance Team may be reassigned to another team. The minimum manning would require at least a fully staffed Anchor Team and a fully staffed Insertion Team, with a reduced Surveillance Team. If the contingency is too devastating, then the Task Force Leader may immediately withdraw the Task Force— bringing all their teams back to us in 5000 A.D." Genesis adds, "Within each Task Force, the Task Force Leader constantly moves to the point of greatest friction. In most cases, the Task Force Leader will remain with the Surveillance Team to best direct all operations. But, in some cases, the Task Force Leader may choose to remain with the Insertion Team or Anchor Team depending on scheduled events—like document drops, negotiations with people in the Luminary System, and so on."

"Are there any other interesting details which may be helpful for our readers?"

Genesis touches his chin, then his temple, as he leans back in his chair: "Dogs---"

"Task Forces are getting dogs?" Kai chuckles. It was a funny thing to consider—but then again who doesn't like dogs? The mere presence of the animals tend to lift people's spirits—especially in tough times.

"Yes, it is likely Surveillance Teams and Insertion Teams may have a dog or two."

"To keep morale high?" Kai offers.

Genesis answers, "Mostly for functional reasons, but also for morale. Throughout human history, we have always had a close kinship with dogs—breeding them to be adept in specific tasks. Due to their social nature, several dogs on each Task Force would greatly enhance capabilities."

"How so?"

"Well, just as ancient hunters used dogs to pull sleds, a large dog or two may allow teams to cover longer distances."

"I see."

"Also, a large dog could serve to prevent loss of team members by providing added protection while team members sleep."

"That makes sense."

"It does. We must be mindful of the dangerous situations in which a Task Force is deployed. These team members will have to provide their own security in the midst of an ancient world. In some cases, teams may be deployed where there are no laws and raiding armies move at will. A large dog might only be the beginning of additional security measures, but it is a step in the right direction."

Kai nods in approval.

"The last topic I think I should discuss is Reinforcements. Depending on the length of deployment, the location of the Luminary System and planned dangers which may be encountered, each Task Force may be reinforced with certain specialists and equipment. Dogs are a part of these reinforcements, but they are just the beginning. So, a Task Force can become quite large—a time traveling caravan of sorts, depending on their mission."

The room falls silent as Kai peers down at his notes. As his eyes shift atop the sheets of paper, Kai determines the discussion achieved an adequate introduction to the assigned topic.

"I think that is a good place to stop for now, Genesis. Thank you so much for your time," Kai says with a smile, adding, "And thank you for your willingness to teach our people."

Kai is grateful. He considers the blessing provided by this ancient pilgrim—with wisdom gleaned from battlefields long ago.

Genesis smiles, "Thank you, dear Kai."

<u>10</u>

Future Frontiers— 5000 A.D. & Beyond

Genesis enters the room to meet again with Kai Moschos-Anthropos for the second time. It seems as if a lifetime has passed since their last meeting.

When they last met, the table between them was filled with piles of wrappings—remnants of the food voraciously consumed by the powerful man across from Genesis. However, now the table was a fortress of books: The bulwarks of each stack piled high—each bearing witness of a battle waged for many hours before the pilgrim's arrival.

Genesis peered atop the mighty stronghold separating him and the physically intimidating man on the other side of the table. Kai's eyes no longer darted from side to side—ever looking for another snack. Rather, his eyes danced wildly along the length of the open book before him. His neck craned downward from his massive yoked shoulders as he quickly flapped the pages of the book. His eyes appeared to lick the words off the pages. So heavy was his breathing and the sound of flipping pages, he did not perceive the pilgrim's entry.

Suddenly, Kai is startled, as if physically stumbled on the words before him. He gives out a large *snort* as he looks up . . .

"Hello Genesis."

"Hello again, Kai Moschos-Anthropos, it is great to see you again."

Kai twitches nervously, earnestly desiring to finish what he was reading before his snort beckoned his awakening. Nevertheless, he welcomed this interruption from the pilgrim.

"It is nice to see you too, Genesis."

Genesis answers, "I have been wanting to check back with you since our last meeting. Frankly, I am very impressed to see how different you are!" Genesis smiles. "You look great, my friend."

Genesis' vision is obstructed by tears as he remembers the previous condition of Kai. It appears now the immense human has broken free of an addiction, replacing it with a quest for knowledge—useful knowledge. The pilgrim's mind passes over his ancient past—where myriads of humans were held captive by drug addiction. His heart broke as he reflected on how drugs absolutely destroyed humans in the past—rendering them over time as depleted skeletons of themselves. It was an epidemic of the 3rd dimension—determined to dead end as many humans as possible in the physical world, offering them only a destitute, false vision of spirituality.

In this moment, the pilgrim thought of Kai as a man who broke free of an addiction—using the most successful method of *replacement*. In the past it was noted, quite accurately, that any person venturing to break free of an addiction *must* replace the addiction with something equally consuming—lest they fall back into their old habit of vice. Genesis was most encouraged. He perceived Kai Moschos-Anthropos was rescued from vice as intensive reading and study replaced his presumed food addiction.

Kai gasps strongly as he addresses Genesis in sincerity, "Sorry if I am distracted, Genesis. I have been doing my best to ---." Kai trails off with a snort.

His gasps are most desperate. With each breath, Genesis fears as if it will be Kai's last. This thought, swirling within the mind of the pilgrim, causes an inward cascading—moving Genesis to ever deepening empathy. The pilgrim is ushered by his empathy to a realization: Somehow he feels as if he is running out of time—that he must move quickly to rescue Kai. Genesis had a knack for perception. He would often note how he could hear things before they made a sound—which was the smallest example of least consequence. However, he could also sense the shifting of events leading to disasters and injury. And it was these greater examples of his past, where he failed to act quickly and was left to witness the aftermath of his inaction, which now compelled the pilgrim to press forward in haste. To Genesis, Kai Moschos-Anthropos appeared as a fish out of water—in the gasping throes of life's end, desiring now to achieve the spiritual transformation which he ever neglected in his past. In these moments, the throes of breath steal away thought—making progress most improbable. Genesis reasoned this to be the cause of Kai's ineptitude in present conversation—as a telling sign of the psychological switching off preceding total black out in the mind. *Now or never*, Genesis thought as the pilgrim convinced himself to imminently attempt the seemingly impossible.

Genesis tarries for now, returning to the conversation. "I can tell you are doing your best, my friend," Genesis offers endearingly. "What have you been reading?"

"Well, about . . . places," Kai states inquisitively—as if he is not sure and is somehow lost within himself. Kai pauses, then lumbers through his thought, "Luminary Systems—places I have never been, or I guess don't really remember."

"That is great, Kai," Genesis replied. "I love learning about Luminary Systems. There is so much to discover." Genesis pauses as the swirling within his mind slows. Genesis continues, "Kai, I know we are scheduled to talk about Frontiers today. So I can go over some of my notes with you. Who knows? You might learn about another topic you would like to research."

"Deal! Thank you. It will be nice to listen and give my eyes a break," Kai snorts.

"Alright. Recently our people developed the habit of referring to society challenges as 'Frontiers.'" Genesis reflects, "I have always enjoyed this word because it sounds mysterious. Calling something a 'frontier' is catchy and draws our interest. It makes us automatically beg a question: *What is this frontier?* The lack of specificity is neat. Moreover, in my last life, a 'frontier' reminded people of the journey made across vast expanses as they made new roads, farms and cities," Genesis continues, "So today we still have frontiers. No matter how advanced humans may become as a society, they will always have challenges and community goals. This is the case with us today."

Kai snorts. Genesis thinks he may have something to add. After waiting a moment, the pause becomes awkward, so Genesis continues . . .

"A 'Frontier' is something which poses a problem for humanity. By confronting Frontiers we help humanity to make true progress. I am convinced I was allowed to time travel so I can prevent the downfall of humanity. My past experiences give me perspective on what needs to be accomplished."

"Genesis, that makes sense. We should all think about who we are because that will give us clues on what we should do," Kai adds. It is a simple and remarkable observation.

"Yes, Kai. If everyone thought about their past, then used their own knowledge and talents to help others, humans could move forward together."

Kai manages a slight smile as he breathes in sharply, "Genesis, what are some of the Frontiers we will face?"

Genesis answers, "First, *helping humans to become 4th dimensional* is a Frontier faced by humanity. There are many today who haven't stepped out of the 3rd dimension for themselves. It is possible for 3rd dimension humans to move onto the Luminary Watchhand, but they need a 4th dimension escort. I would like to see us focus more on spiritual teaching to help people reestablish those personal connections once maintained by people in the Bible."

Genesis speaks further, "Another Frontier will be the *establishment of 5th dimension time travel* within our society. As this emerges in our society, we will need to provide safeguards for people. Although this is theoretical now, it is likely that 5th dimension time travel will have some dangers—particularly with Dead Ends. This would make it similar to the 4th dimension danger associated with people reaching Luminary Systems without a retrograde to escape. I think the 5th dimension may pose similar problems which will need to be managed. And, just as some humans need to serve as guides for the 4th dimension to prevent people from getting stuck at Dead Ends, I am certain we will need advanced 5th dimension guides. But in the case of the 5th dimension, I believe we may need angels—actual angels—to help us. This is an exciting possibility, but due to my research into Jacob's ladder and the Bible, I think the 5th dimension is one primarily used by God's messengers, also known as 'angels.' Upon reaching this Frontier, the main effort will involve the retrieval of humans from the past.

"After the establishment of our 5th dimension ability, humanity will face the Frontier of *ancient visionary recruitment*. We will need to train Task Forces to go back in time to retrieve specific skilled individuals—in addition to defining ethical criteria for recruitment. For example, we will not want to snatch a person off their timeline without their permission. Nor will we want to take someone during certain stages of their life. Ultimately we need to define procedures to ensure we are being most respectful and that we are identifying people with the skills we need.

"The *incorporation of lost ancient skills* will present a series of Frontiers. For example, if an ancient visionary possesses a lost skill, then the full incorporation of that skill within humanity as a whole will become a Frontier akin to how we are currently trying to get all humans to become 4th dimensional.

"Moving forward, the *establishment of 6th dimension capability* will be another Frontier. My concept of the 6th dimension is based my ancient Israelite research, where I believe many Bible prophets achieved 6th dimension capabilities during their life. These prophets include Zechariah, Daniel, the author of Revelation, and Joseph in the book of Genesis—along with many others. At this time it may seem as if we are still far away from achieving movement into the 6th dimension, but I think we may partially break into it soon. Specifically, within this dimension, I am certain we will bring resolution to many of the physical maladies which have afflicted humanity throughout its entire lifespan. In this dimension I believe we will encounter those who have been incapacitated in one way or another in the 3rd dimension—who I refer to as Wanderers. And in this way, great healing to humanity will take place in the 6th dimension. The healing is so vast that it will connect us in a moment to all human history—allowing us to reach back in history to undo pain suffered by humans.

"The 6th dimension will likely contain Wanderers—many, many Wanderers. The *integration and restoration of Wanderers* will be a Frontier within itself—as it will be necessary to help Wanderers gain physical dimension capabilities in the case that their incapacitated physical bodies are located elsewhere in humanity's past. As we arrive within the 6th dimension we will find these Wanderers will be very advanced spiritual humans. Due to the challenges posed with Wanderers it will be most prudent to have procedures in place so we are not caught unprepared. In the 6th dimension we will have these

186

advanced spiritual humans teach us about higher dimensions as we help them retrieve and repair their broken physical bodies.

"The *7th Dimension and beyond* will present further Frontiers. Due to the miraculous transformation of humanity I predict in the 6th dimension, I cannot fathom what the 7th dimension and beyond could be. But I am certain there is more beyond the 6th dimension. Indeed, no matter how far we venture forward, God Himself will always be greater. So, I wager eternity itself will be a vast journey of challenges and discovery—even after complete morality and perfection is achieved for all the redeemed.

"And, of course, Kai, there are Frontiers already present in the 3rd and 4th dimensions around us. Specifically, *the Luminary Systems* themselves are uncharted Frontiers for which we will need exploration Task Forces. Our maps are incomplete and there are many regions where we have no data. And, within each Luminary System there is likely an entire system of flora, fauna and resources which need to be studied. Then we need to define environmental conservation procedures so none of these areas are misused.

"Moreover, *the 4th dimension Luminary Watchhand and the Outer Darkness plane* are Frontiers which should be charted. There would be value in exploration Task Forces moving out as far as they can from every possible jump point on the Luminary Watchhand to provide an exhaustive list of Dead Ends and a complete retrograde schedule from each Luminary

System. In itself, this would serve as an incredible, yet necessary task. Concerning the Outer Darkness, it would be good for teams to explore it on its surface. This would be a bold task when considering the drastic rise and fall of the plane itself to terrifying heights, but I think this 'should' be charted. We should gather data on the terrain itself, in addition to designing equipment for travel—perhaps water, track, wheel and hover vehicles, or combinations thereof. Why do you ask is this important?" Genesis rhetorically poses to his counterpart, "To have data in the case of contingencies. It would be most prudent to have trained Quick Reaction Forces who can perform rescue missions. Frankly, we never know as a society when we may be required to move into the Outer Darkness. Maybe in the 6th or 7th dimensions we might need to retrieve Wanderers from these regions. So, if we are diligent to prepare for this Frontier now, we will be prepared when those potential contingencies arise."

"Wow, Genesis. You will need some brave explorers to go out there," Kai snorts as he reenters the conversation.

"We surely will. That is indeed a Frontier because we have no idea when we will need to do rescue missions. It is good for us to prepare diligently now, as we have opportunity to prepare, rather than waiting for a problem to arise and being totally incapable of action."

A moment passes.

When considering the hope contained in all these Frontier prospects, Kai Moschos-Anthropos feels enthusiastic. In fact, he is overtaken by enthusiasm. . . .

Suddenly Kai's lungs have a renewed vigor—as if a great weight has been removed from his chest. He breathes in . . . deeply, very deeply . . . and clearly— incredibly clear, so very clear.

The snorting and cloudiness of mind which captured Kai a moment earlier seems to have vanished. In this present moment, Kai falls silent, as his mind swirls within its newfound clarity—attempting to discern the depths of the transformation within which he seems to be finding himself. He feels awakened as his mind reboots. He sees the pilgrim before him, the books to his right and left, and the ceiling above him.

Kai, thinking of the Outer Darkness plane, recounts the joke spoken many sessions earlier by Genesis.

Kai jests, "Genesis, do I still get to take a flashlight and batter---"

Kai trails off at the realization of something quite peculiar. As he repeats these words, his mind swirls with foreign memories—each being claimed in order, one at a time by his conscious self. Kai *Leon*-Anthropos, sees the pile of snacks on the table in his mind. Then a parade of memories, moving at first in single file . . . then in a rush.

He was somehow present in all those interview sessions—although he couldn't have been. *Could he?*

Kai's mind merges within itself. His breath quickens and his vision tightens. The walls stand up and march toward him. The ceiling and floor are drawn toward the table—as with hidden cords. Everything collapses inward upon Kai as the pilgrim places his hand upon his shoulder. As Genesis rejoins his hand across the room, the walls shatter, then melt around them.

Kai mentally shakes himself free from everything as the ox, lion, eagle and human become one. In a flash he sees rows of half-bubbles beneath him. Kai breathes in. Then he steps forward.

In a moment, Kai Leon-Anthropos was awakened as from a dream. In that same moment, his mission began.

Final Reflections

Dear 21ˢᵗ Century Reader,

At first, I intended to abandon readers at the conclusion of my book as they struggled to understand both Genesis Pilgrim and his interviewer, Kai. However, as I reflected, I realized this would be a disservice to readers, as it is unlikely anyone would be able to sort it out. So, here is my explanation (which I hope you will enjoy) . . .

Concerning the characters in <u>Interview with the Time Traveler</u> . . .

Even in this futuristic society, Genesis Pilgrim is a man of spiritual power. He does not interact with people merely within the 3ʳᵈ dimension reality. Rather, he directly interacts with the minds of other humans— helping them to awaken from themselves. This is a paradox. Although Genesis is a physically broken man, and even psychologically broken by battle in his past life, it is that brokenness from which spiritual power grows. Although we may each possess power and gifts, we all need someone to help us. Genesis exemplifies this principle. He can help others, but he also needs compassion and mercy to sustain him.

Genesis Pilgrim achieved 4ᵗʰ dimension capability through PTSD depersonalization and derealization in the same way as David in the Bible. (For more information on this

193

topic, read my book: <u>Dear David: Learning to See God through PTSD, Anxiety and Depression</u>.)

Although this book seems to be a series of 10 separate interview sessions, being conducted by four different "Kai" interviewers, the 3ʳᵈ dimension reality is that there is only one Kai, one interview and one physical interview room. During the interview, Genesis is individually addressing different rooms of Kai's mind on different dimension levels.

Kai is a 3ʳᵈ dimension human who desires to become 4ᵗʰ dimensional. His goal: To lead the first team back in time on the first time travel mission by futuristic humans. So, although the interview centers on the teachings of Genesis Pilgrim, there is a 4ᵗʰ dimension process which is occurring below the surface. As Genesis is asked questions, he is busy at his real task—helping Kai to emerge from the 3ʳᵈ dimension prison within himself so he can become 4ᵗʰ dimensional. In the interview, Genesis uses his 4ᵗʰ dimension abilities to separate Kai from himself—addressing the different dimensions of Kai.

In the first chapter, Genesis attempts to do the 4ᵗʰ dimension transformation within the 3ʳᵈ dimension inner-person of Kai Aetos-Anthropos. However, in this first session, Genesis finds the eagle personality of Kai to be jovial and unprepared for transformation. Thus, Genesis abandons his interaction with this part of Kai's mind.

Then, in the second chapter, the 1ˢᵗ dimension of Kai is the ox character, Kai Moschos-Anthropos. The pilgrim addresses this most basic aspect of Kai—supposing the problems with Kai's 3rd dimension aspect may be rooted in his 1st dimension self. In Genesis' first session with the ox-man, Kai is distracted by food—with the many wrappers on the table. Although progress is made, this shows the ultimate transformation of Kai will not occur in his 1st dimension.

So, Genesis causes the lion-human, Kai Leon-Anthropos, to emerge in the third chapter. He finds within this 2nd dimension personality of Kai an eagerness for advancement. So, the spiritual work of Genesis within the mind of Kai centers upon the pilgrim's development of Kai's lion personality. Genesis spends two long sessions with the lion in chapters 3 and 4.

Then, Genesis re-engages with the eagle personality of Kai in chapter 5—checking to see if there have been improvements since their first session. Considering that the 3rd dimension of a person corresponds with the eagle, Genesis allows himself to cry in front of this aspect of Kai. This accustoms the 3rd dimension of Kai to observing pain, and learning how to move into it at opportune times to bring healing. Thus, the pilgrim transforms the eagle's jovial nature of inputting jokes into a desire to input healing into situations he will later observe.

Genesis determines there has been progress, so he re-addresses the lion personality for one more detailed session in chapter 6.

Then, Genesis causes the 4th dimension aspect of Kai Anthropos-Anthropos to emerge in chapters 7 and 8.

Finding Kai to be ready to attain 4th dimension awareness, Genesis spends the last two sessions with the eagle and ox personalities in chapters 9 and 10, respectively. The goal is for the pilgrim to make a final assessment of each. In the last session, Genesis discovers there has been a grand advancement within even the lowest dimension of Kai's personalities—the ox. Whereas the ox previously was consumed in gluttony, the ox now is consumed with the pursuit of knowledge and self-discovery. Although the ox is incapable of fully understanding due to dimensional barriers, Genesis is compassionate. He speaks with the ox-man as a father would gently guide a beloved child.

Thus, the two-fold purpose of the interview is complete. Genesis offered explanations for his readers, while simultaneously beckoning forth Kai from his 3rd dimension mind. While speaking with the ox personality of Kai, Genesis causes a grand transformation to occur within all four personalities. Kai realizes suddenly he is all four personalities. In that moment, Genesis oversees the break of Kai as he achieves 4th dimension capability. And, in remarkably circular fashion, the title of this book in its conclusion applies equally to Kai as it does to Genesis: Both are time travelers who are being interviewed.

Kai gets his wish—becoming a time traveler who is immediately sent back in time. Genesis Pilgrim is revealed to be an Angelic Conduit, perhaps the only one in 5000 A.D.—capable of sending humans back in time through the 5th dimension. But, the question will become: Will Genesis find a way to bring Kai back to 5000 A.D.?

In a deeper sense, Kai is connected with the Bible passages of Revelation 4:7 and Ezekiel 1:10—each portraying the unification of ox, lion, eagle and human. In my later works, this connection will be developed further. The Greek word "kai" can be translated as "and." This is the first clue within the text—indicating each interviewer is a component of a shared identity. Then, the Greek surnames of the separate Kai characters each correspond to the respective dimension each represents: Kai Moschos-Anthropos is the 1st dimension ox; Kai Leon-Anthropos is the 2nd dimension lion; Kai Aetos-Anthropos is the 3rd dimension eagle; Kai Anthropos-Anthropos is the 4th dimension human.

The 10 interview sessions are at first mysterious. Genesis caused Kai to perceive these shifts as a side effect of pulling each personality to the surface. The different items on the table are a part of those shifts in perception—where the books and the snack wrappers are mere props within Kai's mind as extensions of the personalities themselves. The individual rooms where the sessions took place were corridors within Kai's mind— while his physical body remained with Genesis' physical body in the physical interview room.

Last, did Genesis place his hand upon Kai's shoulder once or twice? Indeed, as a part of Kai's emerging depersonalization he could have caused the single hand placement to be shattered into two different perceptions—each with a specific purpose. Within the hand placement is found a clue pointing toward the powerful supernatural shift which occurs in Kai as he fully claims his 4th dimension self. Within the merging of the two hand placements is found the reality of the mind. If you are a person who enjoys these types of books, you may enjoy attempting to reconcile the two hand placements found in the book as a brain-teaser.

Overall, the awakening of Kai in this book gives us hope. It teaches any human can awaken to the spiritual nature around them if they desire to do so. For Kai to step outside his 3rd dimension cage, he merely needed to commit to doing so. Then he left behind the things which hindered his awakening. In this case, the 1st dimension aspect of Kai was held captive by his addiction to the things of the world, and his 3rd dimension self's lightheartedness prevented the determined resolve to break free.

For any human to emerge from the 3rd dimension prison around them, they must simply commit to breaking free from the physical things which hold them captive— whatever those things may be. God provides the strength when we provide the willingness. We must choose to walk by faith, not by sight (2 Cor. 5:7).

I hope you enjoyed this book as much as I enjoyed writing it. Farewell until next time.

In Christ,
Genesis Pilgrim

Terms Referenced

Publication Instructions

To: Task Force Leader
From: Accessions Commander

Message: Upon transcript receipt, ensure dissemination using current methods. Ensure assigned grids maintained under constant surveillance. Remain prepared for all document drop retrievals.

Last, provide feedback in dedication concerning location of document retrieval. If we receive your message via past document research, that specific drop point will be assigned priority for future drops.

Godspeed,
Genesis Pilgrim, Accessions Commander